AMBER J. KEYSER

POINTE, CLAW

carolrhoda LAB
MINNEAPOLIS

Carolrhoda Lab™
An imprint of Carolrhoda Books
A division of Lerner Publishing Group, Inc.
241 First Avenue North
Minneapolis, MN 55401 USA

For reading levels and more information, look up this title at www.lernerbooks.com.

Quote on cover from *The Log from the Sea of Cortez* by John Steinbeck.

Cover image: © Eugene Mynzul/Alamy.
Interior images: © autsawin uttisin/Shutterstock.com (claw mark); © RubberBall/Alamy (dancer); © Joe McDonald/Steve Bloom Images/Alamy (bear).

Main body text set in Janson Text LT Std 10.5/15.
Typeface provided by Linotype AG.

Library of Congress Cataloging-in-Publication Data

Names: Keyser, Amber, author.
Title: Pointe, claw / by Amber J. Keyser.
Description: Minneapolis : Carolrhoda Lab, 2016. | Summary: "After eight years of separation childhood best friends are reunited. One is studying to be a professional ballerina, the other has a rare disease that is rapidly taking its toll" —Provided by publisher.
Identifiers: LCCN 2016006114 (print) | LCCN 2016031843 (ebook) | ISBN 9781467775915 (th : alk. paper) | ISBN 9781512408959 (eb pdf)
Subjects: | CYAC: Best friends—Fiction. | Friendship—Fiction. | Ballet dancing—Fiction. | Diseases—Fiction. | Zoonoses—Fiction.
Classification: LCC PZ7.1.K513 Be 2016 (print) | LCC PZ7.1.K513 (ebook) | DDC [Fic]—dc23

LC record available at https://lccn.loc.gov/2016006114

Manufactured in the United States of America
1-37452-18599-9/19/2016

For my parents,
who raised me fierce

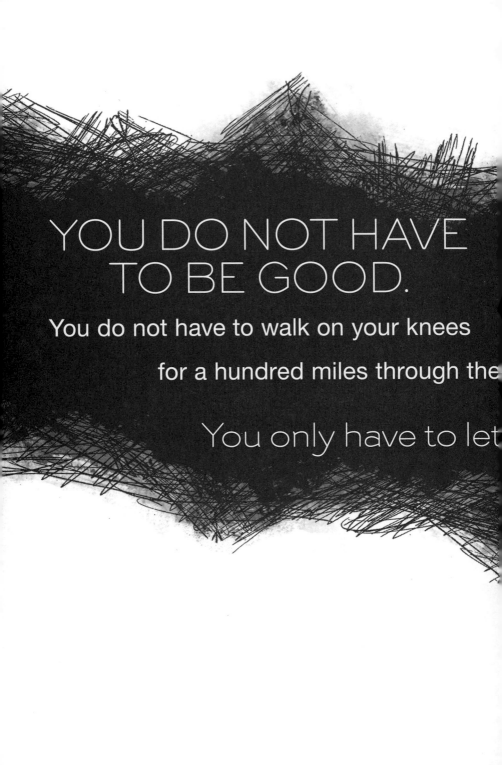

YOU DO NOT HAVE TO BE GOOD.

You do not have to walk on your knees

for a hundred miles through the

You only have to let

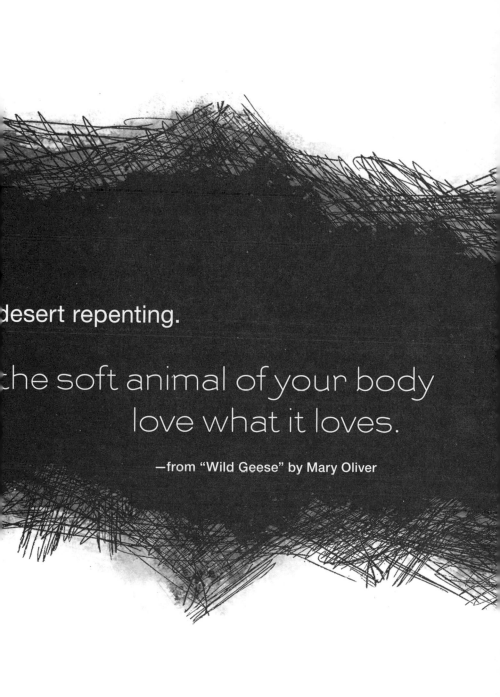

desert repenting.

the soft animal of your body
love what it loves.

—from "Wild Geese" by Mary Oliver

DAWN

I punch a hole in the wall of my room. Through the drywall. White flakes speckle dark blue paint. I tear down posters of women soccer players and Denali National Park and a pod of whales in the gray waters of the Arctic. Everything feels out of reach. The house grates against my flesh. If I don't get out of here I will . . .

What?

Die? Explode? Disintegrate?

My knuckles are white-dusted. My tongue darts through parted lips. My senses absorb everything. The knife-sharp scent of broken capillaries. The plasticine flavor of water-based paint. The dirt-dry parch of chalk dust from the cracked dry-wall. The way the light changes. Or rather, the way my perception of the light changes—the blues and greens brighten, the reds and oranges fade, my vision takes a backseat to smell. I hear more.

This is how it always begins.

I slide the window up as far as it will go and hoist one leg over the sill, reaching with my toes to find the slatted wooden patio covering that shades the lawn furniture below. The edge of the window bites into my crotch. The rough wooden boards scrape the bottom of my foot. I barely register the sliver of wood entering my heel. I'm almost gone when there's a knock on my bedroom door.

My mother.

"Are you all right? I heard a crash."

I look at my right fist, a few drops of blood seeping through the drywall dust. I want to lap them up.

"Dawn?" she says.

And I remember my name.

If I don't answer my mother, she will come through the door. She will clutch my arm, drag me back into the house. But I need to go, so I climb back through the window and try to find a voice.

"Nothing wrong with me." The words are more croak than language.

"Are you sure you're okay?" she asks, and I know she is pressed against the locked door, straining to discern how I have disappointed her this time. I try to ignore the scents that pummel me—her perfume, the fertilizer the neighbor spread on his lawn, the dog two doors down who is marking a tree, and most of all, the fecund musk that has called me to wander. I push it all down so that I can answer as she expects.

"It's fine," I say. "Clock fell on the floor when I snoozed it. I'm going to sleep a bit more."

I feel her hesitation, and I'm not sure how much longer I can keep it together.

Finally, she says, "I'm going to the gym to work out. Back in a few hours, okay?"

"Sure thing," I say.

She waits a moment longer in the hall, and then I hear her take the stairs two at a time, eager to get away from me.

As soon as the garage door rumbles, I pick my way across the patio covering, climb to the top of the six-foot-tall, good-neighbor fence, and jump down into the soft dirt below. The subdivision where my mother and her husband, David, live is right on the edge of the urban growth boundary. Behind the always green, always clipped lawn, on the opposite side of the fence, is a wheat field.

This is where I crouch, on the edge of a sea of new shoots.

The sky is a slab of gray. No rain. Not yet. But these clouds are nimbostratus and that means rain is coming. Besides, it's March, in Oregon. Rain.

Months from now, in August, when the wheat is tall and golden, the farmer will harvest and great clouds of dirt and wheat dust will coat the windows. My stepfather will complain about having to hire the window washers. He'll say he didn't pay top dollar for golf course living to have to smell diesel and be on the wrong end of a wheat stalk.

What he really means is that it galls him to live this close to poor people.

On the far side of the field is a three-mile-wide swath of forest. It's dark in there, even during the day, and redolent of night rot and fungus. Tucked among the Douglas fir and western red cedar are trailers and falling-down houses. Blue tarps cover leaking roofs. There's a guy with old dishwashers in the ragged patch that passes for his front yard. A woman does manicures out of her house. During the school year, kids straggle out of the woods and board the bus with torn coats and last year's backpacks.

The kids from my street call them dirt munchers.

But that's where I'm going—into the forest. Because I have to know what is making that smell. The tang of it overwhelms my other senses, drawing me forward. My vision dims. I slide back into my limbs, run across the field. My bare feet sink in the rain-softened soil. I smell the wheat roots writhing through it, a wet odor that entwines with the oily, rank scent I am following.

On the far side of the field, I cross the road. The gravel nicks my soles.

I lose the scent and pause, trying to find it.

There it is again—biting, calling, leading me into the forest. I give in and follow the smell. I cut behind half-fallen-down houses and an RV on blocks. It is critical that I notice landmarks. Chicken coop. Rusted lawn mower. A backyard garden.

I am going to go dark.

This is how it happens.

My senses change. My muscles burn. My joints seize up.

Each time, I wake, not from sleep but from something else, in a place I don't remember going. Twice in the last week. Five times in the last thirty days. Nineteen times in the last twelve months. Landmarks are required.

I keep running through the trees until I get to the edge of someone's property. It's fenced—chain link. My fingers clench the wires so hard that both hands hurt, not just the one that punched the wall. I'm barely holding on to consciousness.

I inhale animal musk, damp earth, the acrid smell of urine.

The reason for my presence here pushes against my temporal lobe. This confusion is the worst. How can I stay ahead of my mother and the doctors if the order of my mind decays? I cannot let that happen. Through observation, I will elucidate my purpose.

The fence is bent and rusted.

To my left, I catch a glimpse of gravel road, the front property line. The name on the mailbox says *Hobart*. There are signs everywhere:

No Trespassing

Beware of Dog

You're In My Sights

There's a dented truck with no tires and a broken axle, angling into the dirt. The single-wide trailer doesn't look much better. Probably leaks when it rains. I go to the right, tracking the perimeter, feeling the ache in my muscles and wondering how far I walked to get here. I see a few sheds, metal-roofed and tilted out of plumb. More chain-link fencing.

That's where I need to go. The urge of it presses the air out of my lungs.

I drop on all fours, crawling next to the enclosure until I find a loose section, a gap between fence and ground. I widen the opening enough to squirm through on my belly. There's trash everywhere. Empty oil bottles, crumpled cans, parts of machinery I can't identify, rolls of decaying carpet, a huge pile of moldy straw soiled with animal waste. The scent of each item prickles, repels. Yet the undercurrent is there, the deep, fertile, liquid smell of . . . I don't know what.

I push to my feet and pick my way through the wet, overgrown grass toward the dilapidated sheds. Another circle of fencing.

That's where I need to go.

The ripe, bestial pull is too powerful to resist. I am hungry, and there is so much wanting. I'm on the edge. I'm getting worse. Can't let it happen now. Must know what calls me. Data will keep me present. Facts, science, quantification. I estimate the dimensions of what I can tell is a cage, twenty feet by fifteen.

The ground: packed dirt. Non-animate contents: a pile of dirty straw, a water trough, a pan of what looks like dog food.

And in the middle of the cage is the one. Wilddarkhuge. Living, breathing, pacing. My heart bangs ferociously against the bones of my chest. Adrenaline sparks through my limbs. Nothing prepared me to find this animal here in the shit and the trash and the decay.

Ursus americanus.

The animal in the cage is a black bear.

Its head swings toward me in slow motion, a planetary movement, gravitational. Its eyes, her eyes—I don't know how I know she is female, I just do—are small and cinnamon-colored and set close together. Her fur is more than black. The dark is undershot with auburn. Her muzzle is golden, honey-colored on the sides, darker on the top. She watches me. I cannot look away. I don't want to. Her gaze draws me in and down and through the muck of this place to another. Open sky, distance, a flight of geese; a fenceless, cageless, roadless expanse. An unraped wilderness deep enough to hold the whole of her, of me, of us.

I want to fall into her vastness.

She smells me, huffs, grunts.

I am enveloped in the redolent scent that called me here. I sink into it, this smell that speaks of the hunt for berries, a rotten log full of grubs, spawning salmon.

She is:
three hundred pounds, muscled
needs territory, ten square miles
runs thirty-five miles per hour
average lifespan, eighteen years

I am:
one hundred forty-seven pounds
five feet two inches tall
two days into my menstrual cycle
sixty-four days away from my eighteenth birthday

My edges begin to dissolve. I hunger to fit my body into hers, to shed this skin that binds. To cut the lock. To walk away. But the bear is caged.

As am I, in this flesh that constantly betrays me.

JESSIE

I'm here early, the first to claim territory at the barre. I need time to coax my muscles into submission. Six days a week, six hours a day, I am here at Ballet des Arts. There is never a day when my body does not throb with pain.

The front wall of the studio is mirror. The right wall is floor-to-ceiling windows, facing the street. It's March. The gray sky cups the city in cloud hands. Outside, people in raincoats rush by on their way to work and school. Some pause, look in. Their eyes tumble across my body, and I feel exposed.

I fold in half at the waist. My head hangs loose. My hands are limp against the polished wood floor. I breathe through the fiery stretch behind my knees, smelling dust and rosin and the sweat of all the dancers who have inhabited this room. When I stand up again, a gray-haired, gray-suited man older than my father is running his eyes over me. I tug my black leotard farther down my ass and and look away.

Lily arrives next.

There are only thirteen of us in the intensive pre-professional program at Ballet des Arts in Portland, Oregon. At fifteen, Lily is the youngest and, if I'm being honest, the best.

The arch of her foot en pointe is delicious—neither too soft and prone to injury nor too flat. There's a fluid grace to the way she moves through space. Her lines are perfect. Every bone is the right proportion. On top of everything, she is actually nice. Amazing that she's survived the Ballet des Arts wood chipper this long.

She comes into the studio and drops her dance bag against the back wall. She always wears her dark hair in a low bun at the nape of her neck. Her skin is a deep, tawny brown that looks amazing next to her yellow sweater. She peels off layers until she is dressed just like me in a black leotard and tights.

I hold on to the barre and swing my legs, first one and then the other, in wide circles to loosen the hip sockets. Through the windows in the back wall of the studio, I can see the foyer, empty now but sometimes occupied by parents or younger students watching us rehearse. On the other side of the foyer is the office where Tamar, the head of our pre-professional program, is on the phone, barking at someone about coming in to tune the piano.

I sit next to Lily and scissor my legs wide, leaning forward until my chest is flat against the floor. "We're in for it," I say. "She's already mad."

Lily puts on her ballet slippers. "Same old, same old."

I draw my feet together in a butterfly.

The studio fills. The others pile their bags near the piano. These girls have come from all over the place to dance in Portland. Mimi flounces in. She's from Paris but did most of her ballet training in London. Nita's right behind her with a few more of our crew. She sits down next to me.

"Stretch my feet?" she asks, straightening her legs. I kneel in front of her and take her left foot in both hands, pulling it out, then downward, curving her toes toward the floor. "Hurts so good," she sighs as I switch to the right foot. "You next?"

I nod and present my feet.

The joints crack and I groan. "You sound like an old lady," says Nita, grinning at me. She's from a family of performers. Her dad plays the oboe in the Cincinnati Symphony, and her mom used to tour with a classical Chinese dance company before she moved to the States.

"I feel like an old lady," I say as she hauls me to my feet.

I like Nita and Lily, but I can't afford to like them too much. There will be two company spots opening up at the beginning of the summer. The artistic director, Eduardo Cortez, will choose two dancers from among us to fill them.

Once we are in the company, we'll start at the bottom—corps de ballet. We'll become dancing snowflakes or flowers or sylphs. Our job will be to match each other as exactly as possible, to be the backdrop against which the prima ballerina shines. We will become part of a string of girls cut from construction paper, hands linked.

But for now, I have to stand out.

Friends would get in the way.

Franz, our pianist, arrives. He's only in his twenties, but his pale hair is thinning. If he catches us alone, he smooths it over the top of his head and whispers about all the things a musician's fingers can do.

Tamar, having decimated the piano tuner on the phone, strides from her office to the front of the room and claps us to attention. She may have been one of the greatest prima ballerinas to come out of Israel, but to us, she is all drill sergeant.

"Plié, plié, grand plié. In first, second, third, fourth, and fifth." Tamar snaps her fingers, and Franz begins a four-count intro.

We assume our positions at the barre encircling the room.

Tamar paces, counting in a clipped bark. "And grand plié. One, two, three, four." As I finish the movement, I press the ball of my right foot into the floor and slide it out to the side. The instant I settle into second position, I feel Tamar behind me. She jabs one red-painted nail right below my left ass cheek. "What's this?" she snaps. I stretch taller and focus on wrapping the muscles of my inner thigh to the outside. "Better. Watch your turnout, Jessie, and I won't have to look at that bulge."

I finish the grand plié in second position. When Tamar has moved on, Nita whispers, "You've got the bulgiest bulge."

I move into fourth position, managing not to laugh, and glance around the studio. Each and every one of us is whip-thin and flat-chested. You can't get this far in ballet if you're not. We live in fear of extra padding. Even Caden, the only boy in the program, is bulge-obsessed, compulsively tucking his junk so that it is there but not too there. "High def is not your friend," he claims. "No one needs to know if you're circumcised."

We finish on the first side and use Franz's transition measure to turn. Right hand on the bar, I'm now staring at Nita's back. Tamar counts her way past me. No finger jab. I imagine pushing my toes down through the floor as I move into second position. In the window, I see a thin reflection of myself superimposed on a homeless woman and her heaping pile of shapeless bundles.

Third position.

Two more women walk by the window. One is a dark-skinned woman with the kind of bulges men like. She sways past on skyscraper heels, not bothering to look in the studio. The other is covered head-to-toe in black. Through the slit for her eyes, I can tell she looks our way.

To her, I must look naked.

The combination repeats in fourth and fifth positions. Plié, plié, grand plié. It is the most basic exercise we do. I have been doing pliés since I was nine years old. Day in. Day out.

Sweat begins to trickle between my two non-bulges.

Franz plays another transition measure, and I rise on my toes, turning, catching myself in the mirror. I could be a pale pink figurine spinning a slow pirouette in a music box. I adjust my neck and chin. I twist muscles in my forearm, my upper arm, at the top of my elbow. Countless sinews working together will make my arm look boneless, weightless, made of the curvature of the earth.

We hold the final position.

Even motionless, my muscles quiver with effort.

Franz lets the last notes fade and looks up from the keys.

As soon as the music is gone, the dancers around me stretch and preen.

In the mirror, I catch Franz staring.

We move through the barre work without a break. I've been in the program since last fall, and the warm-up exercises are always the same. Tamar saves her creativity and most of her criticism for when we are doing center practice without the barre.

By the time we begin the grand battement, I'm totally focused on maintaining apparent ease—a Tamar requirement—while sending my right leg rocketing toward my nose. I critique each movement in the mirror. Don't clutch the barre. Fix that chicken neck. Suck in the bulge.

When it's time for us to battement to the back, we all turn toward the barre so we won't kick the person behind us. I launch my right leg until it is nearly parallel with my back. Tamar taps my right shoulder. Somehow it has inched up toward my ear. I command it downward and battement again. She grunts her approval and moves on to stab her red nails in Nita's direction. When the exercise is finally over, she grants a water break and with a theatrical wave of one arm summons us away from the barre so center practice can begin.

Tamar teaches us an allégro combination, all fast footwork and speedy legs. She urges Franz to push the tempo faster and faster. By the end of it, I can barely catch my breath. Nita puts her head between her knees. Lily pants delicately like a cat.

The slow, sustained movements of adagio induce a different kind of agony. I slide one foot up the inside of the leg I am balancing on and unfurl it in front of my face. My thighs burn as I move the elevated leg to the side and then to the back. Holding the final arabesque, I check my line in the mirror.

The brushstroke running from my extended right arm through my body and ending in my elevated leg is not quite right. I adjust, find the balance point, and stretch into the arabesque. The piano music softens and wafts over us. I pull through the arabesque, drawing my leg forward into the final pose.

Tamar nods.

Acceptable.

And says, "Again."

"Wanna grab lunch?" Nita asks as she picks a piece of dead skin off her big toe after class. "I'm craving a gyro from that food cart by the art museum."

I stash my ballet slippers in my cavernous bag and layer on a long-sleeve T-shirt and hoodie. "I brought lunch," I say, holding up my brown paper bag. "I'll stay here and wait for pointe class."

"Be that way then," says Nita, leaving me curled on the couch at the end of the foyer. She tugs on Caden's arm. "How about you? It'll be a date. You know you want to date me."

"Always have," he says.

"I knew it!" Nita crows.

Caden grabs his things and heads for the men's dressing room on the opposite side of the foyer. "I'll be ready in five."

The idea of any of us dating each other is ludicrous. We're more like brothers and sisters than potential partners for sexy times. And really, thirteen almost-siblings forced to compete the way we are is a formula for Armageddon, not teenage love stories.

But we do like each other. Mostly.

Brianna I can do without. Watch her in class and she is always calm water, smooth and effortless, but she can make a drama out of any fucking thing. From the women's dressing room, I hear the she-devil herself. "You mean, you didn't know?"

She emerges from the dressing room with her posse hanging on every word.

Mimi, who is Brianna's bestie, says, "Do you really think Selene slept with both of them?"

Brianna's voice drops to a whisper. "That's why Eduardo wants to get rid of Vadim. So he can have her all to himself."

Nita pipes in with the sarcasm she excels at. "It's a global ballet conspiracy."

"I heard she screwed the artistic director when she was in Boston," says Brianna, ignoring Nita.

Lily winces. She's pretty religious—Sundays at church, Christian homeschool—and always gets a pained expression on her face when the girls get nasty.

"That's a rumor," I say. "Nothing more."

"You're naive," says Brianna.

"And you're so worldly, your highness."

Brianna scowls at me.

"What I think," Nita tells Brianna as the whole noisy lot of them heads out of the studio, "is that you watch too much porn." Brianna's protestation of innocence is too loud to convince any of us. Caden trails behind, hanging on every word.

Lily smiles weakly at me before she heads out the door. Her mom always picks her up since she thinks our idle hands will lead to trouble in paradise or something like that. Through the glass front door, I watch her get in the car, unable to remember the last time my parents set foot in the studio. They are not, shall we say, aficionados of the ballet.

I'm not being fair. I know that. They pay for my lessons and the never-ending supply of pointe shoes. They come to every performance and bring me flowers. They're proud of me. I know that too. But I also overheard them talking about how college will broaden my perspective and how glad they'll be when this ballet phase is done.

Ballet phase.

Their words, not mine.

How can something that is everything be a phase?

I think of Lauren and actually feel sick. She was one of us until last December when she fell during a rehearsal for *The Nutcracker* and blew out her ACL. Just like that, she went from dancer to nothing. I ran into her downtown a few weeks ago and hardly recognized her. She'd put on weight and had boobs straining against her sweater and made a halfhearted joke about how Percocet was the best thing that ever happened to her.

I get out my phone, put in earbuds so I can listen to a podcast, and pull the foil top off my maple yogurt. The front door opens and Franz comes in from his cigarette break, smelling of smoke. "You like the cream off the top," he says, running his tongue across his upper lip. "I knew you were a girl who would go for that kind of thing." He grabs his crotch. "I've got a few minutes before I have to play for the next rehearsal."

I pull the spoon out of my mouth. He's actually got a hard-on. From where I am on the couch, the bulge is head height. "You're gross," I say.

He shrugs and heads into the studio. "If you get bored, you know where I am."

A giddy ragtime tune jostles and bounces out of the studio. Franz on the piano is a wonder. Franz with a boner in his pants is not.

The door opens again.

This time I'm the one staring like a wanker.

It's Selene, the principal dancer of Ballet des Arts.

The best ballerina in a decade, according to the framed *New York Times* article hanging on the wall across from me. I have read it a dozen times. Selene—*pinnacle of achievement in classical ballet.* Selene—*who, through her craft, has achieved singular domination among her peers.* Selene—*unforgettable, magnetic, bewitching.*

Selene walks through the foyer with the splayed, liquid gait that ballerinas develop after many years of constant dance. If she notices me, huddled on the couch with a bag of cashews, I can't tell. But I notice everything about her. The tiny mole on the side of her neck. The tendril of dark hair escaping her bun. The way that from a distance, she appears birdlike, but up close, she is steel swathed in black Lycra.

When she enters the studio, the ragtime stops.

"Thank you for staying to help me rehearse," she says to Franz.

"Absolutely," he says, without a trace of oil. "I'm happy to play for you."

Who wouldn't be?

Through the open studio door, I watch her prepare her feet for pointe shoes, taping toes and tucking soft puffs of lamb's wool into place. When the ribbons are tied at her ankles, she stands and goes to the barre. "Just a couple of warm-up exercises, if you don't mind," she says to Franz. "The usual plié, tendu, battement jeté. No need to stop in between."

He plays the four-count intro that I know by heart, and Selene does the exercises I have done every single morning for nearly a year. Her feet in fifth position are parallel lines. Her turnout is impeccable. Her leg moves as if it is not even attached to the rest of her body. And her feet. God, her feet. They are curved like the moon and sinuous like waves.

Watching her feet takes my breath away.

As soon as she has completed the three exercises, she moves into the center of the room, and like a paper clip to a magnet, I get off the couch and stand at the viewing windows. The first bars of music begin. One leg extends directly over her head, and I swear the earth stops spinning.

I can't breathe.

She's that perfect.

It's like she is the reason ballet exists.

When her leg sweeps into arabesque, I am released and air fills my lungs again. She is impossible science, weightless and infinitely dense at the same time. I drink her in. My throat tightens with longing. I want to look like Selene. I want to dance like her. I want to touch her. I am desperate for some alchemy that will transform me into her. When she finally swirls into the last, dying bars of music, my eyes are wet with wanting.

DAWN

I wake in pain.

Graysky, flat as metal. Mistdrizzling. Trees tall, trees press, trees all around.

Time has failed. Again. I check my wrist—bare. How long was I gone? A few hours, maybe. Definitely the same day because my stomach does not rumble. There is a vague memory of climbing out my window. There is a sliver in the bottom of my bare foot.

It takes a long time to find my way back to the house I live in. I climb the fence to the yard, leave streaks of mud on the boards of the deck. I can still smell the bear. She clings to me. The cage gnaws at my bones.

The pull of her.

The tightness of the enclosure.

It's tinder, a spark, the beginning of violence.

It burns in me, even as I walk through the back door and into the house.

My mother is sitting at the granite island in the kitchen, tapping her perfectly manicured fingernails on the sides of her coffee mug. Always tapping. On desks. On tables. On the steering wheel of her SUV.

She is:
five feet four inches tall
one hundred ten pounds
honeyblonde from a box
well-preserved, as they say

She takes in the muddybloody feet, the wet clothes, the stench of me, and begins to shake, apoplectic, red-faced. "Oh god, did it happen again?"

Again, again, again. Yesithappenedagain.

This mother, my mother, she sells BodyBeautiful™. Home-based business. Pyramid scheme. She recruits downlines for uplines, applies face cream for frownlines. She lives BodyBeautiful™. They say: *Love Yourself First*. She doesn't like it when I joke about masturbation.

"What happened to your eye?" she demands.

I test them, blinking, both together and then right, then left. The color palette has righted itself. The yellow mug in her hand looks yellow. My voice cracks on the way out. "Eyeswork."

Her gaze rakes over me. "You look terrible."

After I've gone dark, my muscles ache, and I have to reach for words. "Uglytireddirtydaughter."

She winces, regroups, plasters a benevolent expression on her carefully made-up face. "Did you forget that we have an appointment?"

"No," I grunt, pouring coffee, spilling on the counter.

She slides my cell phone toward me. "You didn't take this. You aren't wearing a watch. How exactly did you plan on getting back here in time for us to leave and not be late?"

I shrug.

"We have to leave in fifteen minutes."

She taps the face of her watch and her lips tighten. They are coral-colored like her nails, like her purse. The color of an abandoned skeleton of calcium carbonate. *Corallium rubrum.*

"Are you going to change?" Her tone is careful. She implies that she doesn't care whether I change or not, but we both know the truth.

"No," I say. General policy of refusal.

She stares into the bottom of her coffee cup like it will reveal the solution to the problem that is me. But I realize my jeans are half-soaked, and my feet are bare, and I'm getting cold so I give in. I slug back the rest of my coffee. "David home?" When she shakes her head, I strip out of my jeans until I'm standing in muddy footprints on the immaculate tile floor in boys' boxer briefs.

"I would be happy to take you to Victoria's Secret," she says as I go upstairs.

I change into another pair of identical jeans and clip the chain of my billfold to a belt loop. When I go into the bathroom to wash the mud off my hands and feet, I see the eye. The white of the left one is a crimson starburst of exploded capillaries. Looks like shit, but at least it's evidence for the doctor to see.

Yet another doctor.

I hate the way I need them.

My mother slides into a long wool coat the color of deer skin and checks her lipstick before heading to the garage. She drives, tapping her coral-colored nails on the shifter. She doesn't let me behind the wheel anymore. The rain beads up on the windshield. She turns on some motivational speech by one of her BodyBeautiful™ gurus. I watch the windshield wipers, flick-pause-flick-pause.

Two months ago, I went dark at thirty-five miles an hour.

You CAN have the life you want.

After that my mother took my keys.

Each day is an opportunity to step toward or to step away from your life's purpose.

David bitched about the repair bills for weeks.

The only one in charge is YOU.

The medical complex is on a hill high above the city. My mother takes the curving road like she takes everything— as if it was made for her and her alone. BodyBeautiful™ blares on. *Surround yourself with things that bring you joy.* Youhavegottobefuckingkiddingme. When we reach the circular pull-through in front of the building, I say, "You can drop me off. Go grab a latte or something."

The sound she makes means *not a chance.* What she says is: "I'll keep you company."

"Suit yourself," I say, because she always does.

In the pursuit of fixing me, we have been to many doctors.

My mother fills out the forms.

My mother does the talking.

I sprawl on a couch in Dr. Cresswell's waiting room, wishing I were anywhere but here.

Going to all these doctors began with the wandering.

At twelve, she found me three miles from home, asleep in a dog kennel with a mastiff. At thirteen, I had to call from a bus station in the next town over. At fifteen, I woke up in a broken-down farmhouse in the middle of nowhere. When she came to get me, my mother had to step over meth heads in her pristine heels. Afterward she took me to the hospital for a rape test.

Negative.

Her fear: having the wrong kind of daughter.

My fear: never finding home.

One doctor said attention deficit and prescribed Adderall.

Another suggested a head injury.

My high school counselor insisted I was a user.

When the wanderings and the forgetting began to co-occur with muscular weakness, they checked for and ruled out multiple sclerosis. When the pain began, they considered shingles, Guillain-Barré syndrome, and fibromyalgia.

Dr. Cresswell is an endocrinologist.

Another specialist for the list.

A nurse ushers us into an exam room. Whitesterile and oppressively clean. The doctor comes in. My mother is perky and hopeful and believes in medical authority. "Dr. Cresswell," she says. "It's nice to meet you. This is my daughter, Dawn."

His hand is cold against mine.

He smells like lemon drops and menthol.

There's a reddish tinge to his nose. Either he's an alcoholic or has a cold.

Dr. Cresswell's gaze lingers on my eye. "Subconjunctival hemorrhage," he observes. "When did that happen?"

"I don't know."

"It was like that this morning," my mother says. "But it was normal yesterday."

She is very fond of that word.

She would like to use it more often with respect to me.

"Have you been coughing or vomiting?" he asks.

"No."

"Straining in any way? Perhaps excessive weight lifting or use of an inversion board?"

This is an item I have only ever seen on late-night infomercials. "Do people actually use those things?" I ask.

"It's not medically recommended," he says.

"Will her eye be okay?" my mother asks, and I have to wonder if she means my vision or my looks.

The doctor nods. To me, he says, "Have a seat on the exam table." He pats the white sanitary paper, and it crinkles.

"Do I need to take my pants off?"

My mother makes a strangled sound.

Dr. Cresswell makes a sound like Santa Claus, an indulgent ho-ho-ho-little-girl chuckle, and presses a stethoscope against the flannel over my left tit. He moves it to the back, sliding it down inside the shirt. Cold hands. Cold metal. He does not comment on my lack of bra.

"Deep breath," he says.

I breathe.

He palpates the glands in my neck, looks under my tongue. He asks me to lie down and presses his meaty fingers into my armpits. There's a deep, painful throbbing in my joints and a burning sensation skitters across my skin when he touches me. Dr. Cresswell must read this on my face because he asks, "On a scale from zero to ten, what's your pain level right now?"

"Zero," I lie because what is the point? When a girl has unexplained pain, it must be in her head, right? My mother, however, is quick to explain. She wants answers.

"It comes and goes," she says. "Sometimes she complains of aching joints. Other times, shooting pain down her arms and legs."

The good doctor mmm-hmms at her.

"My ears never hurt," I offer.

My mother frowns at me, begs me with her eyes to be good, to be respectful, to be un-embarrassing. Dr. Cresswell sits on the rolling stool and types into the computer perched by the exam table. "I see you started menstruating at twelve. Are your periods regular?"

I nod.

"During your cycle, do you have a lot of discomfort? Cramps? Headaches? Moodiness?" This last question he addresses to my mother.

She flashes a BodyBeautiful™ coral smile. "She's seventeen."

Like that explains everything.

"I've been through the records you sent," he says. "Intermittent weakness of the limbs. Short-term memory loss. Intermittent pain. It's an unusual set of symptoms."

Translation: this girl likes making shit up.

This is why I lie to doctors. General policy of obfuscation.

I don't respond, but my mother does not like being patronized.

"Unusual, yes," she snaps. "That is why we are here. So you can shed some light on the situation. My daughter is suffering."

And so are you, I think.

For a moment, I ache to be different, to be what she wants, to fit.

Somewhere.

Anywhere.

Is that really too much to ask?

He rolls backward, holds his palms out. "I'm sure that she is perceiving discomfort. She's a bit overweight. That's hard on the joints. I'm going to order some blood work so we can check her hormone levels, and I think you ought to see a gynecologist to rule out endometriosis."

Dr. Cresswell clears his throat.

"You know," he says, leaning toward my mother. "Difficult menstruation can explain all her complaints."

My mother stiffens. "Having been a menstruator now for many years, I beg to differ." He dips his chin in deference to her tampon expertise, but we both know he doesn't mean it.

"Women often—"

My mother interrupts him. "I had been under the impression that you were something of a specialist."

She knows how to stab. I admire this skill, especially when the target is not me.

Dr. Cresswell purses his fleshy lips. "In the past twelve months, you've taken her to seven specialists, none of whom has found anything more dramatic than slightly elevated red blood cell counts and a vitamin D deficiency. Have you considered drug testing?"

The molecules of muscle—myosin and actin—contract, fire, tense, and I'm off the exam table so fast he flinches. "I'm not a drug addict," I snap. He eyes my balled fists, and I force my fingers to uncurl. Losing control here would not end well. Dr. Cresswell opens the door to the exam room. To my mother he says, "I suggest a psychiatrist."

I want to take my uterus out and throw it at him.

My mother jams her Coach bag in the crook of her elbow. She gestures me out the door in front of her and does not bother to stop and talk to the receptionist who calls after us. She mutters all the way down the hall and into the elevator. She jams the down arrow so hard I expect it to crack.

When the elevator door closes behind me, she snaps. "Idiot."

My rage is replaced instantly by a bloom of warmth. I remember this feeling. I remember being tucked inside the circle of her arms. I remember fitting there—perfectly. It has been so long since she and I were on the same side.

"I'm sorry," I say, not sure if I'm apologizing for losing my temper in the doctor's office or for the distance between us or for being the way I am.

She touches my arm, leaves her hand there.

A connection.

A touchpoint.

A pinprick of what I felt with the bear—connection. It pulses through me, an ache that has nothing to do with the pain of my body.

In the car, I cling to the belief that my mother still holds a place for me. My delusion lasts almost all the way home.

Almost.

"Let's stop and take David to lunch," she says, already taking the exit to my stepfather's office.

The buoyancy I felt in the elevator dissipates, and I slump into my seat. "Let's not," I say, knowing it won't matter, knowing exactly who gets top billing when David is around.

She makes a little sucking sound with her lipsticked mouth. "You don't have to be unpleasant."

That does not require an answer. I stare out the window instead. "I'm tired. I have homework for my animal behavior class." For the last two years, I've attended Stanford University's online high school for advanced students. Pass this course and I graduate with a guaranteed spot in the freshman class next fall. My exit strategy.

"Since when have you needed to study?" she asks.

At least she continues to believe in my intellect even if the rest of me is a disappointment.

"Dr. Kerns wants us to read a bunch of scientific papers before the discussion group."

"You'll be fine," she says, waving me off. "Lunch will be nice. We can eat at that Korean barbecue place you like."

This is revisionist history. It's David's favorite. Not mine.

She parks the car in front of David's office, leaves it idling, and texts him that we're here.

Under the azalea bushes, a flock of house sparrows forages in the bark mulch. Two males with their white collars and black throats fly at each other, locking claws in midair. They fight while the females peck around for seeds and the occasional spider.

"They're not supposed to be here, you know," I say.

My mother releases the sigh she's been holding on to. "What are you talking about?"

I point to the birds. "*Passer domesticus.* House sparrows. Introduced from Europe."

"They're birds, Dawn."

"Invaders," I say, as I watch David push through the door.

David is:
sized to dominate
prone to self-exaggeration
a collector of things that will make him look refined
an overestimator of his own intelligence

David does not have a confidence problem. He waves to my mother, strides to my side of the car, and raps on the window. He jerks a thumb toward the backseat, and I get out and move. I watch the fighting house sparrows when he leans over to kiss her.

"You would not believe the day I've had," he says, moving his seat back until I have barely an inch of leg room. "The deals are flying."

"That's great, honey," my mother says as she drives out of the parking lot.

"How was the appointment?" he asks, not glancing at me.

"Inconclusive."

David lays a big hand on her thigh. "All these doctors can't be wrong. What she needs is a normal routine. Regular high school with football games and prom. You know, the good stuff. This online academy lets her stew."

"I'm right here," I say, hating that he talks like I'm invisible.

"Always underfoot," he mutters.

"David," my mother says, soothing like BodyBeautiful™ AfterSun lotion, "she's bored in regular school."

He grunts, and I wish he'd have a massive coronary blockage. We're at the barbecue place. That should help. David gets out first and opens her door. She says it's the little things that count.

I open my own door.

"She could spend the summer in Alaska with Lars," David suggests. "Get some fresh air. Work on the fishing boat. That'd be good for her."

And good for you, I think, following them into the restaurant.

After my mother's second affair, the one with David, my father moved to Alaska, found Jesus and salmon and a new wife, who is perpetually pregnant.

"We need a diagnosis," she says. "All the specialists are here or in Seattle."

"She has had a diagnosis from multiple doctors. There's nothing physically wrong with her," David counters. "We all know what's really going on."

"She is not mentally ill," my mother says, in a low, curt voice. David knows better than to argue with her. He orders bulgogi. I go through the motions. Open menu. Order last. Chicken please. Sip water. I consider my mother's adamance. Does she believe my symptoms are real or is she mortified by the possibility that I'm a head case?

My father believes my ailments are a problem of faith. He sends missives via text: *Many are the afflictions of the righteous, But the Lord delivers him.* I wonder if he considers me an affliction. My mother pats her hair into place. David orients his chair so he can watch the TV in the corner. Football. Everyone has a god they worship.

My mother turns her attention back to me. "We'll go to another doctor, Dawn. We will figure out what's wrong."

"So you can fix me?"

She looks hurt by the bite in my voice.

"Watch it," David warns.

I don't want to go to Juneau and live with my dad. I don't want to stay here with BodyBeautiful™ and the doctors and David. My limbs feel brittle and empty as if my insides have liquified and drained out through holes in the bottom of my feet. When I go dark, it scares my mother, but it doesn't scare me. Except for not knowing where I am when I wake up. Being no place, at least no place I remember, is better than being empty like this.

As soon as we get back home, I retreat to my room and strip naked. My skin hurts, especially under the waistband of my jeans and the collar on my flannel shirt. My abdomen is puckered with ridged creases from my underwear. I rub them with the palm of my hand. It burns like sand against sunburn. Also better than empty.

I should begin the work for animal behavior. This class is my best chance for getting out of here. The Stanford brochure on my desk is glossy and thick and has palm trees on the cover.

The biology courses include:
sensory ecology
evolution of infectious disease
biotelemetry
neuroethology
biology of hunger
disease diversity
cellular dynamics
neuron death

These are things I want to know. This is my escape hatch, but I'm too agitated to do homework. I pull on sweatpants and a T-shirt, and I pace the room. Ten steps long. Ten steps wide. I'm boxed in. I need a map. Lines on paper. Colors in lines. A description of the world. An origin story. Directions to where I might belong, where I might have come from, and where I am going.

JESSIE

My chest aches. Watching Selene has left me gutted. She is more than body. She is earth turned ethereal. It's the only magic I believe in—the way a body can become something else. When that happens, it erases the uncountable hours in the studio, the blisters, the near constant pain.

I want, I want, I want.

If I'm not chosen to stay with Ballet des Arts . . .

It's a good thing that there is no one in the studio to see me getting all weepy. Pointe class begins in twenty minutes. The others will be back soon, and I need to pull myself together.

I pack away my lunch and pull off my socks. I knead my feet with my hands, pulling the toes up and then pressing them forward until they crack like the clatter of gunshots. My thumbs massage the insides of my arches.

I can catalog my body's shortcomings in detail. Too tall. Slightly too much ass. Feet that need more curve. Legs that need a few more millimeters of hyperextension. It's not that I hate my body. I don't. But I know the way it deviates from the requirements of ballet. Training and hard work are wasted if skeleton and sinew don't meet specifications. Or at least come close.

I am close.

I know that too. I wouldn't be at Ballet des Arts if I weren't.

Nita and Caden push through the front door. Nita is flushed, and he is laughing. "You missed the gyros," says Nita, blowing onion breath on me.

"Brush your teeth," I say, pushing her away.

She laughs again and tries to plant a kiss on me.

"Don't be a cheater," teases Caden as he heads to the dressing room.

"You're my one and only," she calls after him. To me, Nita says, "Do you have any Band-Aids?" She rummages through my bag without waiting for an answer. "I'm using your last one, okay?"

"Sure," I say, pulling the new pointe shoes out of my bag. I can't avoid them any longer. The toe box on the old pair is shot. The satin of the new pair gleams, all peachy-pink and perfect. A wet dream for little girls everywhere.

They will suck to break in.

I bend the new pointe shoes back and forth, trying to force some flexibility into the hard leather shank that forms the sole. The rest of the girls come back too, and soon Brianna is holding court. This time she's on a diatribe against modern ballet.

"It's not even ballet," she groans. "Sixth position is a sham. Call it jazz and be done." She makes jazz hands, and Mimi giggles.

Moving onto my knees, I press the pointe shoes against the wood floor, leaning on them with my full weight. I roll the shoes back and forth, kneading and softening the toe box, which is made of hardened layers of fabric and glue.

They will punish me today. I know it.

"Do you have any Tegaderm?" Lily asks.

I hand her an adhesive sheet of the thin, clear surgical film. She cuts a piece to put over the blister on her middle toe that is swollen with fluid. That way, when it pops, the loose skin won't rip right off.

"That's nasty," I say.

She shrugs. En pointe is brutal. Pain is part of the deal.

I clip the toenail that tends to get ingrown and then pull my tights down over my toes. I pick at a bit of lamb's wool until it's in the exact right shape and slide it into the first pointe shoe. The satin ribbons cross over the top of my foot and again behind my ankle. The knot settles just above the knob of my ankle bone.

I repeat the ritual with the second shoe.

When all of us are finally ready for class, the floor is strewn with the detritus of our feet—crumpled medical tape, Band-Aid wrappers, bits of moleskin, and a roll of thin foam tape.

Lily goes to the barre, where she elevates one leg and rests it on the barre. Slowly, she slides down until she is stretched nearly in two. Nita and I take places behind her, shifting our weight back and forth through our toes, trying to force suppleness into our feet.

Franz comes back from his smoke break.

Tamar arrives, and she is in a mood, glowering at Brianna and the others still sitting on the floor. "It would appear that you do not plan to work today." She snaps her fingers and her nails are tasers. They're at the barre in half a measure. Franz pounds out a foreboding beat that tells me everything I need to know about the class to come. There will be suffering.

After a brief warm-up, Tamar orders us to the center. "One,

two, three. One, two, three. Waltz toward the corner. And arabesque. Hold it. Hold it." Tamar conducts us with raised arms. We rise and fall and hold at the flick of a finger.

I steal a glance at the mirror.

Lily's line is perfect, and her leg in arabesque is far higher than mine. I clench my left ass cheek harder, risking the chance that my lower back will seize up.

"And finish to curtsy," Tamar barks. The music ends, and I rub my back. She tells Franz that she needs something fast for turns, and notes skitter out of the piano. Turns are my thing so I make sure I'm first in line at the rear corner of the studio. We will do the sequence one at a time across the diagonal of the room. Tamar barks out the combination.

I assume fifth position with the heel of my right foot snug against the toe of my left foot. My arms are rounded; my pinkie fingers graze my thighs. When Franz begins the intro, I extend my right leg until it's pointed in front of me. My arms rise parallel to the floor, right arm in front, left out to the side.

I gather force, pin my eyes on a spot across the room.

When the measure begins, I throw my limbs into motion, spinning across the floor. My arms snap open and closed. My head holds the spot as long as possible then whips around to bore into it again. With every revolution my right toe reaches out, finds vertical, claims the center, reaches out again.

Balance.

Momentum.

I am pure physics. Beyond analysis, beyond critique, I am pure body. At the end of the room, I gather it all into a single point of calm and hold the arabesque. Without checking the mirror, I know my line is perfect.

Franz plays a short transition, and the next girl in line gets ready to go. I break the arabesque, walk along the wall to the back of the room, and begin the queue for the next series of turns from the back corner.

Halfway through Lily's turn sequence, the door to the studio opens and a frisson of excitement shivers through the assembled dancers. A dark-haired, bronze-skinned man glides into the room like he is made of the ocean and coconut butter with a pinch of panther thrown in.

Eduardo Cortez—the artistic director of Ballet des Arts.

He will do the choosing for the spots in the corps de ballet.

We are all trying to be exactly what he wants.

He leans against the mirror at the front of the room while we continue. I'm up again. This time flying across space with my left leg in charge of rotation. We finish out the turn sequences and move on to grand jeté, which, like the turns, we do one at a time across the studio. It is a perfect opportunity for Eduardo to evaluate our skills.

It is also an advantage for me. I may be a little too tall for the classical ideal, but it serves me well here. When I leap across the floor in midair splits, people notice.

Tamar puts us back in lines and explains the long adagio sequence she wants us to do. Brianna and Mimi edge closer to the front to make sure Eduardo has a good view. Lily does what Lily does. Perfectly composed, she waits for the cue to begin. Tamar asks Franz to play and puts us through our paces. Eduardo appraises us as if he is preparing to buy a prize thoroughbred, which I suppose he is. We have a lot in common with racehorses. You have to be fast out of the gate and run before you age out.

Eduardo asks Tamar to have us repeat the combination. We hold the long, slow movements in arabesque and attitude until I think my muscles will ignite. My inner thighs, my butt, and my quads tremble and cramp, a deep, clenching pain that I knead with my knuckles between repetitions.

Eduardo stops in front of Caden and urges him into arabesque. He slides two fingers under Caden's leg and lifts it higher, then adjusts the tilt of his chin.

"Perfect," he croons, rolling the *r* and releasing Caden with a nod.

Next is a series of complex combinations that threaten to tie our legs into knots. "Relevé, relevé, relevé," Tamar barks. Exhaustion makes it harder and harder to keep up with Franz's furious playing. In the mirror, I can see the sweat-drenched faces of the other girls. Mine is no better—bright red and blotchy. We smell terrible, and Eduardo's expression is unreadable.

Worrying about whether he likes what he sees makes me muff the combination, and Tamar insists that I repeat it, jabbing her red fingernails in the air like a puppet master. When I finish, she says, "Better," which we all know means *not good enough*.

Finally she gathers us like a bouquet of flowers in the center, and we bend low, dipping our swan necks in the formal curtsy that ends every pointe class.

"I need a moment of their time," Eduardo says to Tamar.

"Of course," she says, but there's a tautness around her mouth that tells me she is displeased.

"As you know, the student spring showcase is coming. As head of the school, Tamar typically does the artistic direction for you as I am busy with the company." Eduardo nods toward

Tamar and continues in his lilting accent. "This year, however, I will be taking a larger role in the showcase."

This explains our teacher's irritation. Turf wars.

"Tamar will be in charge of the younger students as usual, but I will make the casting decisions for those of you in the pre-professional program. You'll be featured in one of two pieces. I am directing one of them. For the other, we'll have a guest choreographer."

His dark eyes sweep the room, commanding this stage. "I'll be making decisions about the composition of the company after the showcase. Consider it your audition and give me your best."

Our best?

Each and every one of us will eat our pointe shoes to be chosen for his piece. Whoever the guest choreographer might be, no one is as important to my future as Eduardo Cortez.

Finally he releases us and I hobble out of the studio. After uncountable transitions from demi-pointe to pointe in my new shoes, I expect my feet to be bad.

But not this bad.

When I take my pointe shoes off, the inner canvas is stained red. The skin of both heels has ripped clear off. Blood wicks up my tights, scorching the pink fabric like flames on tinder.

My mom calls when I'm walking to the MAX train, but I don't pick up.

It stops raining. The sun dips behind the hills to the west of the city. All of a sudden the air is liquid and soft, and it catches the rumbling engines of the cars, muting them. The sidewalks are nearly deserted. When dusk comes like this, surprising and supple, the words for the purple-blue light are ones that fill my mouth—bimulous, gloaming, twilight.

It feels infinite.

I could vanish.

A shiver ripples down my back.

I could vanish and no one would know where to look. This is what happens when you move to a city and live with people you hardly know and dance with girls who only see you as competition.

I'm wearing flip-flops so that nothing will touch the open, bloody wounds on my heels. My feet are lumps of pain. The concrete feels like it's chewing them off at the ankles. I'm so tired my eyes can hardly focus. I settle into my seat on the MAX train and stare at my lower appendages. So much is riding on the right legs, the right steps, the look that will catch eyes and hold them fast. So much is riding on Eduardo Cortez.

And on the perfection of my body.

The energy I've hoarded throughout the day from packets of cashews and turkey jerky and bananas is gone. I try to stay awake as the train judders over one of this city's many bridges. The natives know their names in order. I only know the way to Patrice and Ed's neighborhood.

Five stops before my own, the train empties almost completely. I'm left with a sketchy-looking guy, and I can't help but replay my parents' big city warnings about being alone at night, about listening to my gut, about unspoken things that can happen to girls. As if the unspeaking is a kind of protection. As if cities are the only places where hands grope and grab.

They have cautioned me against wearing short skirts and have given me into the safety of Patrice and Ed, who care for me like a gerbil, tender-ish and distantly affectionate. They leave food out and occasionally fresh sawdust. They let me sleep in their son's room while he is away at college. If Mom and Dad thought there would be supervision . . . well . . . not so much. I don't intend to correct their misperception.

Patrice and Ed are still awake when I get home, drinking white wine and reading on the couch.

"Hello, hello," says Patrice, raising her glass in my direction. "How was class?"

I drop my bag and kick off the flip-flops inside the front door. "It was hard."

"That's good, right?" says Ed.

Patrice drains the last of her wine. "I can't wait to see the spring showcase. Do you know what you'll be dancing?"

"Not yet." These two words plunk down on my shoulder like bird poop, supposedly good luck but also embarrassing and requiring extra laundry. "There will be two pieces in the upcoming performance cycle. I'll be in one of them."

"Are the roles any good?" she asks, trying to sound like she knows something about ballet.

"Don't know that yet either."

Patrice yawns and folds up the newspaper.

"I'm turning in. Coming?" she says to Ed with a look that says she is not quite ready to sleep.

They fight sometimes. Lying awake at night I can hear angry, urgent voices from upstairs. Point and counterpoint. I don't know what they fight about, but in the end, they always have sex. I hear that too. The bed frame pulses against the wall, rhythmic and urgent. Patrice moans when she comes, and Ed calls her Patty.

He carries their empty wine glasses to the kitchen sink. Patrice points me to leftover dinner in the fridge. "You look tired, sweetie," she says.

I nod.

"Are you sleeping okay?"

I shrug. Her brow creases. She's about to probe deeper so I say, "Everything's fine." I don't think she will understand how each day replays itself as I lie in bed trying to sleep. I analyze my own performance, looking for flaws, trying to determine if I am good enough to be chosen.

Patrice is an engineer of some kind. The articles she brings home and leaves scattered on the kitchen table are incomprehensible. Her tiny plastic models made on a 3-D printer look like a cross between bones and robot parts. She's book-smart but incapable of reading my face.

Everything's fine is a lie, but she doesn't know it.

They say their good nights and head upstairs.

I eat alone.

There's a note on the counter that says my mother called. Three messages in two days. It's a record. I won't return this one either. We always have the same conversation. *Ballet is not a career path. Stop now before you wreck your knees. How are you going to support yourself?* The chicken I'm eating turns to cardboard in my mouth. My throat swells, choking down tears or vomit or the truth.

I'm not sure I'm good enough.

I don't think I'll be chosen.

But I've never wanted anything more.

I look at my heels. At nine o'clock tomorrow morning I will go back to Ballet des Arts. I will shove my battered, bloody feet into ballet slippers. I will ignore their screams and dance.

DAWN

Night is coming.

I dress. Loose sweatpants and a boy's undershirt. The sleeveless kind. My nipples show. I touch them, and they harden. I squeeze my tit in one hand, wishing it were someone else's hand. Or that my body were someone else's.

A touch meant for me.

Is that too much to ask?

I open the window. When I do, I smell the bear.

It shouldn't be possible from this distance, but I can. I gulp the scent of her into my lungs and go to my computer and begin to research. Exotic pets. Private zoos. Large mammals. Laws, licensing, animal welfare. Wild capture, captive bred. Declawed, defanged.

The numbers—I need numbers—and I find them.

These numbers eat me alive.

In the US, in captivity, in private hands:
15,000 nonhuman primates
15,000 big cats
2,000 bears
1,000 canids

In pens and cages, in trailers and in houses, in suburbs and hidden valleys, in my own goddamn backyard, there are wild animals in captivity everywhere. The Internet pummels me with images of chimpanzees in costumes and macaques sleeping in baby cribs. You can go to MonkeyMall.com, for fuck's sake. There's a famous actress who grew up with a pet lion that swam in the pool with her and slept on the kitchen floor. *He was a member of the family!*

A woman in California writes from her bear's perspective, putting words into jaws. And the bear says: *I love living in captivity. I'm safe from hunters and I have plenty to eat. My human mommy loves me and I love her.* My stomach heaves. I half expect the next line to be something straight from BodyBeautiful™: *You CAN be the bear you want to be.*

I lean back in my desk chair and let my eyes glaze over. Bluish light from the monitor illuminates my room. Sounds filter through the still-open window. A garage door. Someone coming home late.

I know without a shred of doubt that the bear is pacing, pacing, pacing. I can smell her.

I want to go to her.

I want to bury my hands in her fur.

I want . . .

A dog barks and I remember.

We are eight.
We beg to sleep with the dog.
The dog is two years old. A golden retriever. Her name is Honey.
"No dogs in the bed," says Jessie's mom.
Jessie tugs on her arm, practically swings from it. "We'll put sleeping bags by the dog bed. Pleeeeease," she begs.
Honey licks my face, my ear, my nose.

Her mom gives in. We link hands and race to find pillows and blankets and stuffed animals. We sleep in a nest of limbs and fur. Softness peppered with elbows and the dog's wet nose and her coat making us sneeze and laugh and sneeze again.

I love this dog.

I love my friend.

My Jessie.

I sit at my desk, gulping air.

My mind holds both of them simultaneously. They go together somehow. The bear who I have only met today, and the girl who was my friend, my best friend, my gone friend. The one I haven't seen for eight years. Another wound that is my mother's fault. I'm going dark again, and I don't even care.

Whiffsmell, the air—sharp, ripe, rotted. Effluent. Excrement. Straw.

Poundthrob, drum-throb, ache-crush.

Painthrob in my boneslats.

Pause.

Not boneslats—ribs.

Can't see. Glued shut, eye-gunk. Pry them open. First one. Then the other. Even then can't see. Ohgodohgodohgod. Don't take everything. A choked prayer.

From me . . .

an unbeliever.

Air through pinched nostrils. Sewer fills lungs. Can't mouthbreathe. My jaw is clamped shut by the muscles in my cheeks. Rigor mortis—the stiffness of death. But I am not dead.

I am . . .

trying to put the pieces back together.

Lying on damp dirt. I hope it's dirt.

My eyes come back—the blue tones first. Corrugated tin roof, full of holes. Daylight muted. Cloudheavy with raindrips in the gonebits. Half rotted boards for walls.

I am . . .

named after the first appearance of light in the sky—dawn, dawning, Dawn.

I am in some kind of shed full of rusted-out crap. Don't know how long I've been here. My nails are full of dirt, forearms raw and bloody. I groan when I push to my knees. Joints ache, creak, catch. Moving brings tears to my eyes. The door squeals when I push it open. I hear birds, a faraway truck, a TV mumbling. Familiar smells—dirt, wet, shit, musk, the bear. I am in one of the sheds near the bear. Every sense focuses on her. Need her, want her.

I crawl out of the shed toward the cage, clawing at the shreds of myself, but in my chest, where there should be the heart of a girl, there is nothing. Absence, abcess, worse than darkness. It gapes, this wound. This desperate wound. Its edges are seared and I feel it deep in my body and I want to take the bear and swallow her so that she fills me up again.

It's the empty space that's killing me.

I cannot even cry.

The bear watches me, motionless, the opposite of empty space. I suck air in shallow and rapid pants. Her breath is earthdeep, lowslow, ponderous. I want to bury my hands in her fur and force my lungs to find her rhythm. She knows something I want to know. She's trying to tell me something, but I can't grasp it. Not even a whisper.

Dawn-fuck-idiot.

I catch myself. I catch what I'm doing. I'm no better than that woman on the Internet who shoved words down the mouth of her bear. *My human mommy loves me. I bring the wisdom of the wild.*

This is what they call anthropomorphism: giving human characteristics to an animal. The human brain desires this. It's tricky-slippery that way. But still our species managed science. Somehow. That's the faith I keep, the one that keeps me from crumbling entirely—observation, facts, theory.

I notice:
it is morning
sun in the east
last memory, night
first thought, ohshitno

But the bear, the bear, the bear . . . she consumes me. Is she female? I assumed yes. Must know for sure. Science is about observation. Instinct is something else. The bear begins to pace. I lie on the ground next to the cage so I can look at her crotch.

No testicles.

Female.

Hypothesis confirmed.

She urinates. Steam rises from the stream. There's a rivulet of yellow on the packed earth. It doesn't sink in. Instead it bifurcates. Two rivulets. Another bifurcation in response to a structural anomaly of the ground, bit of gravel here, a ridge of root there. The stream splits again. Even a tiny bit of urine acts like a river, looks like a river when you are a body lying on the ground.

Behind me, the door of the single wide trailer bangs open.

I curl and roll away from the fence, end up on all fours, push myself to standing.

"What in the hell are you doing?!" The man's voice is a bludgeon. He's old and stumping across the distance between us. His hands are knots of wood, the hurting kind. His beard fans out from his chin, a gray and white squirrel's nest.

He repeats himself, eyes still bleary with sleep. "What are you doing, boy?"

"I'm not a boy."

He's not the first person to think this. Short hair, big bones, the thickness of me. I don't care.

His wrinkles deepen, lips-purse, facefrown. "Sure you are."

"I don't think so."

"Why were you lying on the ground?"

"I wanted to know." I spit the words at him.

He scratches his armpit. "Know what?"

"The sex of the bear."

The man tugs at the collar of the dirty thermal shirt he's wearing like it's strangling him. I wish it would. "You're not supposed to be here," he says.

"I can read."

He looks confused.

"The signs. *No Trespassing. Beware of Dog.*"

He grimaces at me, yellow teeth under his stubbled lip. "Who are you?"

"Dawn McCormick."

He waves me forward with one of those gnarled-up hands. "Let's go."

"What's the bear's name?" I demand. My voice rises with every word. "Why do you have her? Is it even legal? I'll report you."

"Goddamn it!" he explodes. "Shut your mouth!"

My eye begins to twitch. The palsy spreads to my cheek. I can feel my whole face twist into a distorted grimace.

"What the hell is wrong with your face?"

"Nothing."

"Nothing, my ass." He grabs my arm in one of those club hands and pulls me along, none too careful. My feet perform a shuffling jig to keep up. Our bodies jostle together, and I smell him. Beer. Spoiled meat. Weed. When we pass his battered single wide, a dog lunges toward us. She's got pit bull in her and maybe blue heeler, some rottweiler. Her head and brindled chest could batter down concrete.

But she's better than the man.

I pull out of his grasp and crouch. She barks once, right in my face, loud enough to set my ears ringing, but then the entire set of her body changes, and I know I can scratch behind her ears so I do.

"Get over here, Bitch," he says, snapping his fingers.

The dog sidles toward him, whining.

"Her name is Bitch?"

"You got a problem with that?"

So many problems. Like the way the twitch has migrated through my arm to my fist and his face could use a hole in it.

"The bear belongs in the wild, asshole."

The old man unlocks the gate, shoves me through it. "I ain't done nothing wrong. Raised her from a cub. Perfectly legal. Now get the fuck out of here."

I see the mailbox, remember his name.

"I'll report you, Hobart."

"You got no ground," he says. "Besides, why would anyone listen to a girl like you?"

The bear has no name.
The dog is called Bitch.
My friend is gone.
I am . . .

JESSIE

Before class, I hand Lily a spray can of Second Skin and lift my right heel in her direction. "Hit me."

"Are you sure?" she asks, tentative, knowing firsthand how much that stuff burns on an open wound.

"On three," I say, leaning into the wall. "One, two, three."

Lily depresses the nozzle, and the sting makes my eyes water. I lift the other foot. "Again."

She sprays me again, shaking her head. Her sweet face swims through my tears, sympathetic, lovely, and young. She has so much dancing in her. Seventeen feels like one foot in the grave. I stretch through creaks and groans, bracing myself for today.

I wait until the last possible minute to put on my ballet slippers. "Where's Nita?" I ask, sliding into a deep stretch.

Lily shrugs. "She has a new boyfriend."

Brianna rolls her eyes. "Probably out doing the nasty."

Franz is cracking his knuckles over the piano when Nita finally rushes in, red-faced and out of breath. It's not like her to be late. It's not like any of us. Late means ridiculed. Late means last. Late means dropped. "You've got like two seconds," I say, poking my toes into the supple leather slippers. They're not even pointe shoes, but it still hurts. Nita sweeps her hair into a ponytail and makes a lopsided bun. It matches her general level of disheveledness. She smells like sex.

Tamar strides to the front of the room. We make for the barre before she begins to yell. Nita is in for it. Tamar senses weakness like a shark smells blood, but maybe her focus on Nita will take the pressure off me and my poor feet. A guilty thought.

We assume the positions for plié and begin. By the second side, I'm not thinking of my feet. I'm in the mirror, looking for error, tweaking the shape my body makes. Barre exercises proceed quickly, and soon I'm covered in a thin sheen of sweat. Tamar has been so preoccupied with picking Nita apart piece by piece that I've escaped without a single jab from those nails. Not true for Nita. Her boyfriend will find bruises the next time they get naked.

Tamar counts us through the barre exercises with military precision. Frappé, rond de jambe, grand battement. She calls for port de bras. We sweep and bend and fold and circle like human origami. I love the feel of taking up space.

Tamar is snapping out the steps for the first combination in the center when the studio door opens, and the collective heart rate in the room leaps into double time.

Vadim Ivanov.

Principal male dancer at Ballet des Arts.

Selene's lover.

Our fantasy.

He's taller than Eduardo, with close-cropped dark hair. A wolf in jeans and a Ballet des Arts T-shirt. It's practically pornography the way he glides to the front of the studio, flips a chair backward, and straddles it. Mimi looks like she might pull an eighteenth-century swoon. Brianna releases a puff of excited air.

Vadim smiles at Tamar and waves for her to continue class.

Tamar gives him a look that would freeze the rest of us into ice.

"What the hell?" Nita mouths when she catches my eye. I shrug and review the steps for the next combination.

For the rest of class, Vadim watches us dance, his presence flustering everyone. Mimi misses her musical cue, and Franz restarts in a huff, pounding the keys to show his displeasure. Brianna messes up the steps.

I try not to look at Vadim, but his eyes have got the shine of animal eyes in the dark. It unsettles me.

Two exercises later, the studio door opens again and Eduardo cuts across the floor, livid. To me, it feels like there is no more air left in the room. An atmospheric pressure change has flattened my lungs.

The two men stare each other down.

"It was not necessary for you to be here," Eduardo says in a tight voice.

Vadim smiles again, predatory. "And yet I am here. Dancing is serious business, yes?"

A grimace twists the corner of Eduardo's full lips.

"Gentlemen—" says Tamar, her face so painfully composed that I think it might crack under the strain. "I am trying to conduct class."

Eduardo chooses to be magnanimous. "Of course. A thousand pardons, Tamar. Continue. I assume my presence will not disturb."

"Or mine," Vadim smirks.

Tamar's only response is a brusque nod, weighty with displeasure.

"Rows!" she commands. "Just because we have *guests* . . ."

The word snarls up in her mouth. "Does not mean that you get to slack off."

We snap to attention—in perfect rows, like dolls in black leotards and pink tights, ready to be moved across a stage.

Eduardo leans against the mirror at the front of the room, crosses his arms over his chest, and assesses us. The hint of a smile lingers on Vadim's face as he too watches from under half-lidded eyes, hungry. There is a battle underway, and it will be fought upon our bodies. I take in the tilt and lean of the girls in front of me. They are already choosing sides. We are willing fodder for the cannons. This is what we want after all.

For the next fifteen minutes, there isn't time to think. Tamar cedes the stage to Eduardo. He wants to see turns—piqué and chaînés and fouetté—and then he wants adagio.

Again and again.

We are all running on fumes, but the girls who don't eat much are suffering the most. Finally, he tells us to change into pointe shoes, and while we change and recover our breath, he focuses his attentions on Caden. We watch as Eduardo asks Caden for a sequence of huge jumps, which he executes like his legs are made of springs. Eduardo ups the ante to a harder combination, offers corrections, and eventually lets Caden relax.

His nod of approval speaks volumes.

There are thirteen of us and one Caden.

One man-boy in tights.

All the ballet studios in the world are full of little girls dreaming of tutus, thousands of us ready to cannibalize each other for the chance to get a nod from Eduardo Cortez. Mimi would throw herself on a burning pyre if she had half a chance.

"Oh, balls," mutters Nita.

Balls indeed. Nita has read the same signs that I have. It's pretty freaking obvious what Eduardo's focus on Caden means.

There's only one company spot up for grabs.

We still have no idea what the hell Vadim is here for. He should be in company class or rehearsing with Selene. I watch the other girls watching him watching us.

When Eduardo is done working with Caden, he pats him on the shoulder. Caden sits and stretches. Instead of leaving, Eduardo leans against the piano with his arms crossed over his chest.

"Is there anything else you want to see?" he says to Vadim.

The wolf stands, gestures us to our feet. "An experiment."

Eduardo rolls his eyes.

We girls feel gravity pulling us toward Vadim. We want his hands on our bodies. We want to be found worthy. Is this how prey feels when it lies between the teeth?

"You," he declares, walking toward me, circling. "You are very tall."

"You are very Russian."

I don't know where the hell that came from. Nerves, I guess.

He laughs, pushing the sound into every corner of the studio. The air that has filled his lungs spills out like vodka and caviar and fur coats.

"En pointe," he commands, wrapping his hands around my waist.

Around us, the other girls step back. I rise. En pointe, I am almost as tall as Vadim. My inner thighs pull forward and flatten. I tuck the heel of my right foot in front of the ankle of my left. I balance on a few square inches of silk, a miniscule point of contact. His palms are fiery through the thin Lycra of my leotard.

"Arabesque effacée."

As I shift my weight to the front foot, Vadim rotates me ninety degrees. I am his to spin or lift.

He chooses lift.

His left hand leaves my waist, and my elevated thigh ignites as he slides his palm underneath it.

"Ready," he whispers, his lips next to my ear.

Without waiting for an answer, he lifts me above his head, and I am weightless. After a moment, Vadim slides me down the expanse of his chest and sets me gently back en pointe. Immediately he sends me into an increasingly complex series of promenades and lifts.

When he is done, the class applauds. I'm pretty sure it's not for me.

He stands back, appraises me as the applause ends. I can tell without looking that the other girls are antsy for their own turn with Vadim. I begin to move out of the way, but he shakes his head a fraction of an inch and I stop.

"Can you do it," he asks, his accent stronger, "like an animal?"

Someone stifles a snort. Probably Nita. But I am frozen in place by the intensity of his voice. It feels like his hands are still on me.

"I . . . I don't know what you mean."

He paces in front of me. "As if your limbs are furred, your claws sharp, and your stomach empty. Can you do that?" he shouts.

I step back. He takes that for an answer. "No? No?" He's in my face. "Why not? If I asked you to be Sleeping Beauty, you would be lovely, but I ask you to be something else, and you're afraid."

There's dead silence in the studio.

Vadim might as well have slapped me.

I danced well for him. I gave him everything he asked for. The steps are supposed to be lovely. That's what ballet is. A girl. Grace. Beauty. All these thoughts ricochet through my head. Confusion must show on my face because Vadim looks disgusted and one of the girls snickers.

"If you can't take any risks, then go back to your mommy," he says.

His expression flays me—contempt, disappointment, dismissal. My mother is behind his eyes. Her disdain. Her admonishment that it is unwise to pin hopes on dreams. His lip curls. He shakes his head. Vadim begins to turn toward the other girls. If I'm not willing there's another girl and another and another waiting in the wings. He is already erasing me.

It hurts.

But pain is a place I know deep in the body.

This body.

It is mine and he does not get to excise it.

"Wait!" I say, suddenly angry. I grab Vadim's hand, force it onto my waist, and rise en pointe. We're eye to eye. "Do it again," I snarl.

This time I move him as much as he moves me. I change my center of gravity. I lean. I shift. My body presses against his. Every movement is bigger, more carnivorous than the last. I abandon precision.

"Yes," he says, straining to put my body where he wants it.

Tension sparks between us. I feel as big as he is.

Bigger.

Every promenade is a battle.

Every spin is a wrestling match. Mine. His. Mine. Never ours. We struggle like animals for dominance.

I never stop watching him. To look away is to submit.

I haven't come this far for that.

When we stop, I make him hold me up.

No one else in the room is even breathing.

DAWN

The walk home hurts so much I wish I were dead, but I still have to climb the fence and get to the window of my second story room because all the doors are locked. By the time I'm back in the house, my muscles burn and my feet are thrashed. My mother would have a stroke if she saw me like this. Purple blooms across my right shoulder. Mud streaks my clothes. There are scratches up and down my arms.

It's never been this bad.

But she won't see.

I'll shower and change, and besides, she never gets any closer than she has to. Doesn't slide an arm around my shoulder. Doesn't squeeze me to her side. I think she's afraid of me.

Correction—

I know she's afraid.

JESSIE

Vadim leaves and class continues. Eduardo doesn't look at me for the rest of the morning. I'm pretty sure he actively avoids meeting my eye. So does everyone else, even Nita. Tamar puts me in the back row during the last few exercises, and I mark the steps stiffly and broken-jointed like the wooden doll from the famous ballet *Coppélia*. When class is finally over, Lily pats my shoulder and gives me the kind of look reserved for funerals.

What was I thinking?

Reckless, incautious, foolhardy. Nothing like me.

I want to slap myself.

It's a distinct possibility that I just dismantled years of training in a few short minutes. Ballet des Arts needs a new ballerina, not a ravening beast.

DAWN

The doctors call what happens a fugue state.

Good student that I am, I have looked it up.

Fugue—

The fragmentation of consciousness. A disturbed mind. The sufferer acts with the pretense of will and intention. Aware, seemingly, of every choice, every movement. Yet there is no recall upon recovery.

The time is lost.

Fugue—

It is also a musical form. A single theme that begins the piece but expands into a series of related musical sequences— imitations, arguments, concessions. They are saying the same thing, but not in the same way. The theme repeats and races. Point on point interwoven into composition.

I call it *going dark* because that's what happens. A curtain falls. Walls close in. There's a black tunnel that buries a point of light.

It is from the Latin. *Fugere*—to flee. *Fugare*—to chase.

This circularity troubles me.

I have been keeping track for the last twenty months. Before that, there are only anecdotal memories. The vague rememberings of a spaced-out girl—the teachers' description, not mine.

But after the farmhouse, the meth heads, the rape test, I began to record with precision. What else are you supposed to do when someone probes you like that?

This is how science works:
make observations
hypothesize explanations
conduct experiments
repeat

For almost two years I have been tracking the fugues, recording what I can remember about when and where and for how long I go dark.

The journal is:
cheap paper with a card stock cover
blue, a color I can see even when the warm tones disappear
three inches wide, five inches tall
white and unlined

I keep it in my bedside table in the zippered bag that holds my vibrator because I know my mother searches my room. I also know she would find touching the masturbation aid far too disturbing to reach past it for the journal. I add an entry for Dr. Cresswell and note that I went dark twice in one day. This has never happened before. Nor has it ever taken so long for me to find language again. And there is something else. My pen hovers over the paper. Something about the bear. It is imperative that I describe this precisely.

I write:
smelled her
wanted her
needed her

The bulk of the bear took me deeper into . . . into what? My mind? An altered state? I don't know how to describe it because I don't remember, but the fugue evoked a memory. Or the bear herself did. I brought it back with me. The memory of Jessie and the dog and the way it felt to sleep tangled together. What does the bear have to do with Jessie Vale? I haven't seen her since I was nine years old. Maybe she's not the one that matters. Maybe what I needed to remember was me, back then, a child with a place in the world. I am positive that the darkness of the fugue is trying to tell me something.

A notification flashes across my computer screen. It's an e-mail from Dr. Kerns, the professor who teaches my Stanford course. I put down the journal and open the e-mail.

From: Dr. Stephen Kerns
To: Dawn McCormick, Student ID # 91967
RE: MISSED SESSION, OB-012 Advanced Topics in Animal Behavior

Ms. McCormick,

You did not log in to the online discussion this morning. Everything okay? I've got to remind you that your participation is required in order to fulfill course requirements. If there are extenuating circumstances that explain your absence, please let me know.

I'm also missing your response to the last assignment. I will accept it until midnight tonight. After that, I have to give you a zero, which I don't want to do.

Dawn, I value the unusual insight you bring to this class and your typically prompt attention to due dates. I understand from my communications with your mother (her initiation, not mine) that you are dealing with a challenging medical condition. I want to help you succeed. Let me know what I can do.

Best,
Stephen Kerns

The extreme niceness of Dr. Kerns oozes out of the e-mail. Fuck my mother for telling him I'm sick. I imagine her words, the way she'd try to make me sound as normal as possible. Implicate epilepsy or an autoimmune disorder. Anything but mental illness. Her fear.

But I'm not losing my mind.

I hope.

I picture myself writing to Dr. Kerns about extenuating circumstances that explain my absence. *You see there's this bear and I go dark and here's my eyeball with its broken vessels and the cuts on my arm and let me tell you how a childhood memory can spill your entrails on the floor.*

It's almost funny.

Instead I get to work on the assignment. I have to make a list of animal activities common to most species.

From: Dawn McCormick
To: Dr. Stephen Kerns
RE: Missed Assignment

This is my list:

obtain food (life stage specific since some animals, e.g., insects, don't feed as adults)

claim/defend territory (optional, maybe better to say find appropriate habitat since barnacles don't exactly duke it out for rock space, or maybe they do; I am not a mollusk)

find a mate (optional given asexual/hermaphroditic repro-duction, e.g., lizards/flatworms/snails)

have/care for offspring (definitely not optional, at least the having part in an evolutionary sense; care is, I know from experience, the optional part)

die

I stare at the cursor, trying to decide if I should delete the last item. Death isn't really a behavior. It's what they call extrinsic: not part of the essential nature of someone or something; oper-ating from outside. Except it happens to all of us eventually. So how is that not part of our essential nature?

I hit Send and my fingers fall from the keyboard and my vision changes—bluish, vivid, sharp. I senseperceive the edge of the fugue and feel as if I could walk toward it or away or maybe stay here in this liminal, in-between space.

See more.

Hear more.

Smell more.

Know more?

Essential: absolutely necessary, extremely important.

Nature: This one is harder. The world—minus man? The world—including *Homo sapiens*? Innate quality, true self, untrammeled reality.

The most real self I have ever felt returns to me.

Another memory.

I go there instead of into the fugue.

We are nine—Jessie and me.

We're in the tree fort.

A cherry tree older than old. I run my fingers over its knobblysilvergray bark and pick out witch faces and monsters in its whorls.

I love this tree.

I love my friend.

My Jessie.

She is a spring sprite, a wood elf, a sparkle, a flash.

When the tree leafs out, we are encased in green rustling. She makes up stories where I'm the hero. We take the parachutes off army men and tie them onto Wonder Woman and Storm and Ms. Marvel and launch them from the highest branch we can reach. We nestle our little girl bottoms into the tire swing and take turns dropping out of the sky. When I am flying, Jessie sprinkles golden glitter on my face, arms thrown wide, and fairy dust dapples my cheeks.

We do not know how little time we have left.

We bask in the essential nature of us.

The memory is so real that I feel like a time traveler. I touch the wetness on my cheeks and lick the salt from my fingertips. The loss is fresh, always fresh, like sea replenished. Shivering, I crawl into bed, curl up into a ball under the covers, and stay there the rest of the day.

JESSIE

The last time I lost control of myself like that was when I was
nine years old and my best friend moved away.

We hold onto each other, tighter than a hug.
Our parents wrench us apart.
It is like being torn to pieces.
We weep for our severed selves.
I cry so hard I throw up in the car. When we get home, my hair
is full of puke and my body convulses. My mother puts me in the
shower fully clothed and turns the water on, ice cold.
To my father, she says, "Look what you've done."
He reaches to her, pleading.
She slaps him hard across the face.
I cry myself to sleep, shivering under the blankets.

DAWN

My mother mixes a BodyBeautiful™ smoothie in the blender. The liquid she pours into her glass is dark green and viscous. It reminds me of bile. "Would you like one?" she asks.

My eyebrows launch off my face, and I open a Coke.

"It's ten-thirty in the morning," she says, frowning at my choice of sustenance.

"That look will give you wrinkles."

She makes a point of looking at her watch to distract from the attempt to relax her face. "We have to leave in five minutes."

David comes in and kisses my mother. Disgusting.

"Where are you off to?" he asks, taking the last of the coffee before I get any.

"Dawn has an appointment at the Zoonotic Disease Center."

The look on his face is priceless. It's like she's spoken Mandarin.

"A doctor," my mother adds.

He only understands small words.

"Another one," he says, looking straight at me. "Why can't you just shape up and fly right?"

I stare back. "I don't have a pilot's license."

His neck flushes above the white collar of his dress shirt. Mad red, not embarrassed red.

"Did you know that there is a parasitic wasp that lays her eggs on the bellies of paralyzed spiders?" I ask.

My mother's lips form a straight line. There is a long pause before David says, "I did not."

"When the maggot hatches, it feeds on the living spider."

"Dawn," my mother warns. "Don't."

David is now as crimson as his paisley tie, blotchy-cheeked and tense.

"Eventually, the maggot shoots a chemical into the spider that makes it build a totally new kind of web. Then the maggot kills the spider and eats it and lives there in the web. Alone."

"I think," he says, in a measured tone, "that you should consider your living arrangements this fall. If I remember correctly, you turn eighteen in June."

My mother grabs my arm so hard her Moon-over-Malibu pink nails dig into me. She doesn't speak until we're in the SUV and she's tap-tap-tapping on the steering wheel. "Why do you do that?"

"Do what?"

She makes a sound like a whale surfacing. "You know what."

I look out the window into this monochromatic, suburban wasteland. Beige house. Tan house. Ivory house. "He provokes me."

Tap-tap-tap. "He didn't do anything."

"His existence provokes me."

My mother inhales through her nose and exhales out her mouth like she's about to go full-*Exorcist* on me. "His existence pays for the roof over your head and the clothes on your back. Such as they are." She sniffs in my direction.

"Maybe I have Ebola," I say, imagining blood running down my face.

My mother is not amused. "You don't have Ebola."

"Have you read up on zoonosis at all?"

"No. That's what the doctors are for."

So much for being an advocate for my medical care.

"I have," I say.

My mother flicks the turn signal with a pink fingernail and grazes her hand along the steering wheel to turn. "Is this supposed to surprise me?"

I shrug. My academic chops are not in question. It's the rest of me that's the problem.

She drives three more blocks before she opens her mouth again. "You're smart, Dawn. A little too smart sometimes. Surely you see that we can't keep going like this."

My whole body goes cold, corpse cold. My tongue sticks in my mouth, frozen in ice. *We can't keep going like this, like this, like this.*

JESSIE

For the rest of the week, you'd think I'd contracted leprosy or been caught shooting up heroin in the dressing room. The other girls give me a wide berth. It reminds me way too much of being at home, where conversation around the dinner table is always careful. My parents say *yes, dear* and *no, dear* and *would you like another piece of bread?* They have perfect diction with zero warmth. They go to bed at separate times. My dad stays up late watching cable news. My mother reads in bed. I've never heard them have sex. I've never watched them hold hands.

But I have seen, in unguarded moments, the pained furrow of my mother's frown. Her discontent.

It poisons everything.

The antidote is self-control, a family value.

At the studio on Friday before class, Brianna holds out her phone with a smirk. "I took a video of you dancing with Vadim." Mimi titters as the YouTube video starts to play. It's a dog humping someone's leg to a hip-hop beat. "After that performance not even *Dancing with the Stars* will take you."

The girls gathered around Brianna laugh.

But I was the only one who felt Vadim's hands.

None of them were pushed beyond pirouettes and arabesques into a darker, hungrier place. Remembering sends a shiver through me. What Vadim did makes me very, very nervous.

"Come on. Forget those bitches," Nita mutters, tucking her hand under my arm. "Tamar will be here any minute."

At the barre, I take refuge, as I always have, in the structure of classical ballet. The procession of exercises at the barre. My body—limbs, muscles, ligaments, tendons, bones. The music—a waltz, a march, a tarantella. For years now, my days have been partitioned into neat compartments—morning class, pointe class, pas de deux practice, rehearsal.

Years of work and it all comes down to the next two months.

It has to be me.

I have to be perfect.

I need to stay away from Vadim.

DAWN

The Zoonotic Disease Center is inside the hospital. The building is brand-new. Sterile even. Ironic for a place that is a gigantic petri dish. My mother treats me like a bag of virulent E. coli, pointing to the hand sanitizer by the door as soon as we enter the office. I'm still reeling from the implication of my mother's words in the car.

What will happen when I turn eighteen?

The infectious disease doctor is as efficient as her name: Lynn Ho, MD, PhD. I like all those letters after her name.

My thoughts:
I want letters after my name
we can't keep going like this
like this, like this, like this

We go to her office, not an exam room. I can't even look at my mother. Dr. Ho shakes my hand. I notice this. She is not afraid to touch me. Maybe I'm not a lost cause after all. I like this doctor.

There is small talk about the weather, the doctor's relocation from San Francisco, and how much my mother loves that city. "So elegant," she says, preferring to talk about anything but my body.

"I see you've had an HIV test," says Dr. Ho, reading my records.

"Negative, of course," my mother says, and I wonder why. Does she assume no one would have sex with me? No one has, but am I unsexable? I don't think so. I hope not.

"And has anyone discussed the possibility of Lyme disease with you?"

Dr. Ho is talking to me, but my mother answers. "No one has mentioned that."

"Ticks," I say.

Dr. Ho nods. "Have you spent any time in the northeast recently?"

"I took her to New York City a few years ago, but that's all."

"There are ticks here in the northwest," I say.

"You're right. Black-legged ticks. But Lyme disease isn't as common here as in other parts of the country. Do you spend a lot of time outside? Camping? Hiking?"

My mother shifts uncomfortably in her chair. Probably she wants me to lie. The wandering is so unseemly. *Not a lie*, says the mother in my head, *a more palatable version*. As if Dr. Ho wants to eat me. As if the truth will stick in her craw. Fuck my mom.

To Dr. Ho, I say, "I think so."

Her face does the opposite of what I expect. It opens, encourages. "Help me understand what you've been experiencing," she says.

"I wander, but I'm not always sure where I go." Saying this is much harder than I expect. It makes me feel naked in front of her.

"There are notes in here about frequent fugue states."

I nod.

"And you have no recall of these periods?"

"No," I say, and I want to tell her about the last time, about how I woke suffused with a sense of connection to the past, but I won't offer that in mixed company.

Dr. Ho turns her attention to my mother. "When you've witnessed Dawn in a fugue state, can you describe what you've observed?"

My mother's posture, always elevated, becomes more rigid. She takes her time smoothing the fabric of her skirt against her thighs. She takes long enough that Dr. Ho pushes.

"You have seen her, haven't you?"

I twist in my seat to watch my mother's face for deception. Why did this never occur to me? Has she seen me? Has she watched? That's disgusting, like watching me masturbate, but if she hasn't . . . Is that worse? That she never cared enough to look for the signs?

Dr. Ho's expression is placid, a cool water face, the kind you'd want behind the controls of a plummeting plane.

My mother's tone is careful. "I have seen it happen once."

We wait.

Finally, Dr. Ho prompts again. "And?"

Those lips purse. Those nails. Tap-tap-tapping on the arms of the chair. Her face is a mask.

But Dr. Ho demands revelation.

My mother's voice hitches on the way out. "I found her . . . the experience, I mean . . . disturbing."

I want Dr. Ho to say *We are expecting turbulence ahead. Please remain in your seat with your seat belt buckled.* What she says instead is: "How so?"

"There were noises in her room. I've heard odd things before, but never like this. They were animal noises, growling and snarling. It scared me. I knocked. I called. She didn't respond." My mother shoots a look at me, almost accusatory. "The door was locked, but I used a toothpick to open it."

My mother can pick a lock.

She opened my door.

Both the violation and the care behind it hurt me. It's like she has laced meat hooks through the muscles of my thighs and chest. There are wire cables connecting me to her and with every word, the tension between us ratchets tighter. It will pull me to her or rip me apart.

"She was rambling around the room, swinging her arms and knocking things over, her chair, a lamp. Her movements were so strange, so . . ." My mother swallows hard. It hurts her to say this as much as it hurts me to hear it. ". . . so inhuman, like she was possessed or something. I said her name and she flinched. She actually flinched like I'd stabbed her, and then she climbed out the window and climbed the back fence and . . ."

The light in Dr. Ho's office takes on a bluish tinge. It begins to happen.

I hear:
music from the waiting room
the snap of a nitrile glove around a wrist
the clatter of a syringe in a sharps receptacle

I smell:
a patient, riddled with rot
isopropyl alcohol
my mother's fear

"She ran on all fours," my mother says. "Like an animal."

I pin my gaze on Dr. Ho's face. It looks like she is underwater. "I imagine that was very distressing," she says in the most soothing voice I have ever heard.

My mother starts to cry in salty rivulets that carve channels through BodyBeautiful™ Pale Peach foundation that is looking greenish. At least to my eyes. Dr. Ho hands her a tissue, and my mother folds it into a triangle so she can use the point to dab. God forbid that her mascara run, that she turn raccoon on us.

Or that I go dark.

Not here, not now.

Dr. Ho turns to me. "Do you remember any of that?"

I start to shake my head but force myself to respond in a complete sentence.

Like a human being.

"No, Doctor, I do not remember running on my hands and feet."

The words come out staccato and monotone, but it is enough to pull me back from the edge. Dr. Ho doesn't look like a mermaid anymore. My mother's face is the right color again. I will record this in my journal when I get home. Twice now, I've been able to stop it from taking me. This is new.

"One of the reasons we're looking at Lyme disease," Dr. Ho continues, as if none of this is out of the ordinary, "is that it manifests in different ways in different people. The constellation of symptoms you're experiencing have, at one time or another, all been attributed to Lyme disease. It's often misdiagnosed as everything from chronic fatigue syndrome to Alzheimer's to mental illness."

I watch my mother clutch at that life ring.

Dr. Ho hands me a clipboard with a sheaf of papers. "I've got a pretty extensive questionnaire for you to fill out, and I'm going to order some lab work. We'll get this figured out." She smiles encouragingly as I take the forms.

"I read up on zoonosis before we came," I say.

"Yes?"

"Some people say a zoonotic virus will be the source of the next pandemic, way worse than the Spanish flu or AIDS."

Dr. Ho's smile fades. "It's possible. Diseases that jump from animals to humans are unpredictable."

"It's an evolutionary experiment. New habitat and all," I say, indicating my own body. "Anything could happen."

"You're thinking like a scientist," she grins. "I like that. College-bound next fall?"

My mother has recovered enough to brag on me. "She's in an advanced high school program that feeds to Stanford."

"Good," says the doctor. "We definitely want to have you shipshape before then."

I think:
my symptoms are a constellation
directions in the sky
pointing ahead
to something I haven't figured out yet

When Dr. Ho is done with us, we stop in the hospital coffee shop so my mother can buy a latte. I groan when she spots Denise Muller and her daughter Harley across the lobby.

"Come on," I say. "I want to get home."

Of course, she ignores me. Denise is my mother's BodyBeautiful™ upline. She records inspiring vlogs for her minions about how to sellsellsell and also find joy and eternal peace through smoothies and facials because: *Goshdarnit, you're worth it!*

"We're saying hello," she says.

"I'm not."

My mother doesn't hide her irritation. "It's hello, Dawn, not fire-walking."

"I'd rather burn the bottoms of my feet off than make pretty with Denise and Harley. They had mother-daughter breast enhancements."

"There is nothing wrong with wanting to look your best," says my mother, giving me the once-over. I'm no Harley. Halfway across the lobby, she begins waving. Denise sparkles at her. They hug in that barely-touching way that neither musses hair nor smudges makeup. Harley acts like she's happy to see my mother and fakes it a bit for me.

"It's been forever since you girls have seen each other!" my mother coos.

I lift one hand, robot fashion. "Hi, Harley."

She sniffs delicately, and tucks a curl behind her ear. "Hello, Dawn."

The mothers jabber about new product lines and the annual convention in Vegas where the gold members fawn over the high-up uplines and discuss how to con newbies into the bottom layer of the pyramid. I mean, show others the way to the light.

I shove my hands in my pockets. Getmethefuckoutofhere.

Harley is better trained. She makes an effort, as my mother would call it.

"How's school?" she asks.

When all I do is shrug, she tries again.

"I'm going to University of Arizona in the fall. I can't wait for sun!"

I look outside the main doors of the hospital. "It's raining."

"I know," she says, sounding like it's a tragedy.

There's an awkward pause, which I intentionally make worse by saying, "So are you getting your vag done now?"

"What?"

I gesture to my crotch. "Some people do that. It's like a face-lift for your labia." I can't help hating her. She's everything my mother wants.

Harley scowls at me. "My dad works at this hospital. He's a radiologist. Why are you here?"

It's a challenge. I take it. I shouldn't, but I do. "I might have rabies."

She takes a step back.

"Yeah, they don't know yet, but all this crazy shit is happening to me. Paranoia, extreme agitation, hydrophobia. Do you know what that is?" Her eyes are darting toward the exit doors. Our mothers are bent over Denise's phone. I keep going. "If a rabid animal bites you, infected saliva goes into your blood. The virus goes to your salivary glands and replicates. Over and over and over. You've got virus everywhere in your mouth." I do a passable imitation of a slavering, froth-mouthed rabid dog. "But the virus makes it impossible to drink. Because if you drank water, you'd wash away the infection and wouldn't be able to infect anyone else. Hydrophobia. Get it?"

Harley's mouth is open, silent-scream style.

At some point in my monologue, the mothers notice something is going awry. Denise is horrified, and all color drains from my mother's cheeks. She makes what I think is supposed to be an apology face, takes a hold of my arm, and hustles me outside.

She maintains composure until the parking lot. "How could you humiliate me like that? After everything I've done? This is why you don't have any friends."

Pain detonates through my temples.

I'm furious, explosive. I'm so angry that the edges of my vision are turning black.

"I had a friend."

She knows exactly what I'm talking about.

But I repeat myself. "I. Had. A. Friend."

"Ancient history, Dawn." She spits the words at me. "You're almost eighteen. Make some new friends. Try once in a while, for God's sake, to be a grown-up."

We are nine.

Jessie's face, wet with tears, presses against my neck.

I cling to her, my fingers clutching at her sweater.

She sobs, a galloping, gulping sound like her heart is bursting.

Mine has already ruptured.

My mother wrenches my arms from around her back.

"We're sorry," Jessie shrieks.

Her dad untangles our legs.

Her wails pierce me. "We won't do it again."

My mother locks her arms around me.

Jessie's dad lifts her bodily into the backseat and slams the door.

My friend's hair covers her face in a tangle as she thrashes. I can't see her eyes, and I needneedneed to see them.

I need her.

I need her.

JESSIE

All day Monday, there are whispers about a feud between Eduardo and Vadim. By the time we're done for the day, it's all anyone can talk about.

"They're fighting over Selene," Brianna sighs. "It's so romantic."

"It's not about her," Mimi argues. "Vadim is trying to get Eduardo fired and take over as artistic director."

"Why would he do that?" Nita asks. "Vadim is already the star of every single performance."

"I heard that Vadim wants the company to be more avant-garde," says Brianna. She makes an exaggerated nod in my direction. "You know, modern stuff, weird dancing."

Mimi pretends she's a rutting dog.

"Ha, ha," I say. "You two are so funny."

Brianna shrugs. "We'll see who's laughing when Eduardo picks his favorite dancers for the showcase piece."

"He'll pick you for sure," says Mimi. She's such a sycophant. Their snark peters out when Lily crosses the foyer and heads out to where her mom is waiting to pick her up. No one wants to admit it, but we all know she's the best dancer here.

I follow her out. I can't take another second of those girls.

"See you tomorrow," I say.

Lily smiles. "Yeah, hopefully it'll turn out well for both of us."

I watch them pull into rush hour traffic and wonder what it would be like to have someone pick me up and ask me about my day and tell me it will all be okay. Kind of nice, I expect.

The MAX train is packed.

I pull my knees to my chest and wrap my arms around them in a corner seat. After a full day of class, my body is weak-kneed and limp, but that doesn't stop my mind from whirring. Tomorrow they will announce what roles we are dancing in the spring showcase. I have to be in Eduardo's piece. I need that. If I can't succeed here, my mom is going to pull the plug, and I'll be working at the Target down the street from my house for the rest of my life.

Two women a little older than me get on at the next stop. They're already laughing about some inside joke when they press their way into the crowded aisle and grab the overhead bar. The curvy one with purple hair starts singing some pop song, and her friend leans in to harmonize. They change the words in the chorus and then dissolve into giggles, pressing into each other. The women kiss, and it aches to watch them. I haven't been that close with anyone for a long time.

My phone buzzes. It's Dad, so I answer it. "Hi, Jessie, how are things going in dance land?" His voice is a little too cheery. I am used to distance from him, and this interest unnerves me.

"What's going on?" I ask.

He forces a chuckle. "Can't I call my girl to check on things in the big city?"

"Portland is the same as ever. All the dudes have man buns."

He laughs for real this time. "I guess I'd better start growing my hair."

"Mom will love that."

No response. The unspoken protocol in the Vale household is that the two of them interact as little as possible even through the intermediary—me.

"So—" he says.

Instantly, I'm on alert. "Yeah?"

"I got sort of an odd . . . interesting . . . call out of the blue today." He pauses. The women get off the MAX train with their hands in each other's back pockets. I wish I could go with them. The next stop is mine. I shift in my seat and hoist my bag over my shoulder.

"From whom?"

"Well—" he says.

"Spit it out, Dad." He's being so weird, I half expect him to tell me Mom has cancer or something. Although probably he'd just wait for her to e-mail me. What he actually says takes the wind out of me.

"Do you remember a girl that you were friends with a long time ago? Her name was Dawn."

My throat tightens. I gulp air, desperate to stuff this choking feeling down, down, down.

"Honey?" my dad says.

"Hold on," I stammer. "Getting off the train."

The brakes squeal, and I clutch the phone in one hand while I push through the crowd. I get off, unsteady on my feet like I'm nine again in a body far too big for me. It's so dark outside.

Do I remember? Do I remember? I want to slam the phone on the ground with remembering.

Holding hands at the roller rink. Chasing geese in the park. Building blanket forts that stayed up for weeks. Her dad's French toast. My mom telling everyone that Dawn and I might as well be twins. Together, together, we were always together and then we got caught and she was gone.

Forever gone.

Always gone.

Traffic whizzes by. The lights set my head spinning. I sit on the bench at the train stop and watch it pull away from the curb.

There was screaming and vomit and ice cold water and the slap and the end of the world.

"I remember," I say.

As if I could forget.

"Yes, well, I thought you would. You two were pretty close." There's a forced casualness in his voice that I don't understand. "I got a call from her mom today," he continues. "Sounds like Dawn has been having a pretty rough time of it. She's been sick a lot. Isolated. Her mom is sort of at her wit's end. Doesn't really know how to help."

"Why did she call you?" I can't keep the anger out of my voice. He was the one who pulled me away from Dawn. He shoved me in the car. He slammed the door. He drove away.

"They don't live too far from where you are. About an hour outside the city. Monica was hoping that you might be willing to reach out. I'm going to text you Dawn's contact info as soon as we get off the phone, okay?"

Again there's an edge, a fissure, a subtext I don't understand.

I am reeling from too much input. The rumble of cars. Exhaust fumes. The sound of a fight from the QuikMart on the corner. Our parents tearing us apart . . . I have never cried that hard in my life.

"Jessie, are you still there?"

"Yeah."

"Will you call her?"

"I'll call her."

"Great, great," he says. Duty discharged. He washes his hands of the whole business. "And, honey?"

"What?"

"For now, it would be best if you don't mention it to your mother."

All of this is coming at me a little too fast. "I don't understand."

He's all hem and haw on the other end of the line. "Let's just say that she and Monica had some issues there at the end, before Dawn's family moved away."

"What kind of issues?"

"Just issues. No need to bring up old wounds. Besides, it's about you girls reconnecting, right?"

"Right," I say. If that hadn't happened, maybe it would be me and Dawn with our hands in each other's pants pockets. Maybe I wouldn't be all by myself in a strange city at night.

I slip past Patrice and Ed with as little conversation as possible. My dad's phone call has cracked me open. Lost things are creeping out.

When we are eight, Dawn's dad takes us camping.

We have our own tent, pitched right next to his, and spend every night giggling in a pile of sleeping bags until he growls at us to Pipe down, pipsqueaks. *Every morning there is frost on the ground, and we huddle near the fire, holding our hands out, waiting for hot chocolate with marshmallows. The sun rises like a hot-air balloon, unbelievably close and bathing our faces in gradual heat. We play Uno and eat potato chips at ten in the morning and make stables for our toy horses—Snowflake and Starfire.*

Snowflake and Starfire.

Her phone number is at my fingertips.

Eight years can be bridged with a single text.

Eight years.

And my dad knew the whole entire time where she was and how to find her.

I begged to go see her after she moved . . . I pleaded and wept for her to come visit . . . The answer was always *no, it's too inconvenient . . . no, your mom isn't up for it . . . no, no, no . . .* When I asked my mother why they had to move, her face turned ugly. "It has nothing to do with you girls."

Eight years.

Gone just like that.

I want to murder someone.

I punch in Dawn's number.

Cancel the call before I hit Send.

I cue up a text message. Hi. It's Jessie. Remember me?

I delete it.

I wonder if it is worth opening this wound. I have the showcase to think about and my future. The last thing I need is distractions. I throw my phone on the bed and take a shower and tend to my feet and I can't stop thinking about Dawn.

With my wet hair wrapped in a towel, I climb back into bed, slide my hand under my robe to cup my breast, and close my eyes. I can almost—almost—be convinced it is some other hand. A hand reaching for me that isn't red-fingered and ready to jab me in my weak spots. A caress. A reassurance—you are here, you are real, you are right.

That's what it was like with me and Dawn, all those years ago, real and right.

Finally, I pick up the phone and dial before I can talk myself out of it.

She picks up on the first ring. "Yep."

One word, hoarse, almost guttural. I wonder if her dad has answered.

"Dawn?" I say.

"What?" she asks.

Not *this is she* or *speaking* or even *yes* and the failure of convention makes me think this was a bad idea.

"Who is this?" she demands.

"This is Jessie."

The sound on the other end is almost a moan.

"Jessie Vale?" she asks. My name transforms her voice. It comes out entwined with such longing that my chest contracts.

"It's me, Dawn. It's Jessie." More silence. "Are you there?" I ask.

"Is this real?"

"I don't know what you mean."

"Are you real?" Her voice rises, cracks, drops to a whisper. "I am losing time. Things don't always add up."

I don't know how to answer so I don't say anything.

"What day is it?" she asks.

"Monday."

"Do you still live in Olympia?"

"My parents do, but I'm in Portland now, dancing."

"Dancing," she repeats.

"Ballet," I say. "I guess our parents talked. Turns out . . ."

"Our parents?" There is no mistaking the disgust in her voice.

"Well, my dad and your mom, I guess."

"Of course," she says, scornful.

I feel like I am talking to a stranger. Dawn has been ripped away from me all over again. "Anyway," I say, struggling to sound normal, "my dad said that you live pretty close to me and thought we might want to reconnect."

God, I sound like a tool.

"Did my mom call him?" Dawn sounds furious.

"Yeah."

There is a long pause. "I guess she gives a shit after all."

I have no idea how to respond to this.

After another moment, Dawn says, "Did she say I'd been sick?"

"Yeah."

"I'm not contagious or anything."

"That's good."

"We were just girls," she says. I grip the phone harder, unbalanced. This conversation keeps changing direction. "They shouldn't have separated us like that. It wasn't fair."

It's the kind of thing a little girl says, but I'm too old to expect fairness anymore. Instead, I ask, "Do you remember camping?"

"I forget the now, not the past."

She's making me nervous. Nothing she says adds up. The pause lengthens, and I do not know what careful, polite thing I am supposed to say now. I wonder if she's losing her mind.

Finally, I blurt, "We made forts for our horses."

"Snowflake and Starfire."

"You remember," I say.

DAWN

My heart pounds and spins and spins and pounds, galumphing against my ribs like it has become unmoored and free to tumble home. Jessie, Jessie, Jessie. Back then, our days were woven tight. Moments unbroken. We fit together. Never sure where I ended and she began. *Peasinapod*, they said. *Practically sisters*, they said. *Inseparable*, they said. Every moment. Every day. None of this splintered time. None of these fractures that assault me. With Jessie, I was whole. What we knew and who we were. All good.

And then it was taken, broken.

And now Jessie has called.

All good.

JESSIE

It's Tuesday morning, and class is not going well. Everyone is nervous about the casting for the spring showcase. Franz pounds the keys on the piano with extra menace. I should be working my ass off, but my body is on autopilot. I'm supposed to meet Dawn today, and I'm so freaking nervous that I can't focus on anything.

Tamar stamps her foot along with the bass notes. The class is in a frenzy as we move into the last big set of exercises for the morning. One by one we launch across the floor, crossing space in a series of leaps.

"Higher!" Tamar says to Nita.

"Point your feet," she snaps at Brianna.

Tamar waggles a finger at Franz to up the tempo. I suck great gulps of rosin-scented air and knead my burning thighs. There's barely time to recover before she orders us to repeat the combination. I screw it up again.

"What the hell is wrong with you?" Tamar snaps.

I'm out of breath and can't speak.

"Again," she says, waving back the other girls and making me correct my mistakes. "Again!"

Finally, she throws her hands up in despair. "Fah!" she cries. "I give up."

I give up too.

My lungs are trying to swallow the sky.

Nothing will redeem me during this class.

I just want it to end.

Tamar is lining us up for the final curtsy when Eduardo comes in holding a piece of paper. A hopeful stir rustles through the assembled dancers. We all know he's got the cast list for the spring showcase. I want to cross my fingers behind my back.

Class concludes and we clap for Tamar. *Thank you for the torture*, we say with our palms.

"A moment," says Eduardo, as if any of us was thinking of leaving. We are glued in place. "I will be staging *Four Variations*. A deeply classical piece. Traditional. Elegant." He paces a slow circle around the room. "Ten. I will need ten dancers." We are holding our breath. He stops in front of Caden. "You will dance for me," he says. Caden nods, blushes, and unclenches his hands behind his back. "And you." He points to Lily. "As for the rest . . ." He runs a finger down the list and reads the names of the other dancers he has chosen.

Nita, Mimi, and I are the leftovers.

Caden and Lily have the grace to avert their eyes. Brianna smirks at me in the mirror. The rest shift uncomfortably. If he doesn't think I'm good enough to dance for him in the show-case, the company spot has slipped through my fingers.

Eduardo calls the three of us forward.

"Vadim Ivanov will be mounting an original piece. His own choreography. You'll be working with him on that." There's a hint of a sneer in Eduardo's smooth voice. "Good luck," he says, but I'm pretty sure he means the opposite. Whatever it is that he and Vadim are fighting over, the battlefield is our bodies, as if our feet aren't bloody enough.

I change out of my ballet slippers as quickly as I can. I have to get out of here. Nita is cursing under her breath and throwing things in her bag. Mimi looks like she is going to cry. Brianna is holding court in a voice calibrated to be overheard. "I don't know what I would have done if Eduardo hadn't picked me."

Eduardo did not pick me.

I squirm into my jeans and slide into flip-flops, fighting back my own tears. My hands want to rip the list out of Eduardo's hands and shred it to pieces. I want to scream. Thousands of hours in the studio. More blisters than I can count. Years of striving for perfection. All for a girl's dream—*Swan Lake, Giselle, Sleeping Beauty.*

And I ruined it in a single moment by losing control.

Eduardo did not pick me.

I am a failure that proves my mother right.

Not good enough, not perfect enough.

I was a fool.

Eduardo did not pick me.

DAWN

We are meeting in Rose Square. There is sun—a miracle for March. Food carts on either side of the block. An array of tables. A giant's chessboard. A fountain. I got here early. My mother dropped me off, and I'm twitchy with waiting and watching. Every time I see a little girl, all bounceandspark, a surge goes through me. Could that be her? Then, joltbamdrop, I remember. We are no longer little girls. And I try to watch the women instead of the girls, but I don't want her to be one of them. They are too careful.

I see her before she sees me. Her brown hair is twisted into a bun at the nape of her thin, pale neck. She's a gazelle in the crowd. Agile, fluid, thin-boned, trailing pink ribbons from the bulging bag over one shoulder. Heads turn to watch her pass. Men suck her down like water. She is beautiful in a way that would please my mother. Smoothskin, pinkfrost, rosehip, amour. A strand of hair escapes and flutters across the bloom of her cheek. She sweeps it behind her seashell ear with long fingers.

She is not the girl I knew.

94

JESSIE

What I want is to lie down in front of a bus.

Instead, I fix my face on my head like a doll. In my family, you never let the cracks show. I hitch my dance bag over my shoulder and make my way to Rose Square.

Dawn stands alone.

There's space around her as if others don't want to get too close. She's dressed like a boy. Her hands are jammed into the front pockets of sweatpants, and her shoulders are lifted in a frozen shrug. She's got a hoodie on, the sleeves up above her elbows, and she is scowling. It's the scowl I recognize. I know the foot stomp that goes with it and the way she used to stare at her mother and list our demands.

Peanut butter and Nutella! Roller-skating! Sleepover!

I approach and her frown deepens. She's a head shorter than me, thick-limbed, and chunky. No makeup, jaggedly cut hair. The years have broadened her face, and her complexion is muddy with freckles. I can't read her face at all, but I can breathe in the scent of her, a musk that smells of damp earth and rot.

She is not the girl I knew.

DAWN

We are magnets facing the wrong way. Reverse polarity. An unbridgeable space between us. I should go before her perfect face and her perfect body ruin the past and the memory of the dog and the tire swing and the two of us together.

It is one of the only good things I have left.

Self-preservation dictates that I should rescue that slim comfort.

But I don't leave.

Maybe I have a death wish.

I talk to her. "Did you know that some people use magnets for healing?"

The corners of Jessie's lips twitch. "That's random," she says.

"Well, it's bullshit," I say, "but my mother would probably jam magnets up my ass if she thought it would help."

Jessie laughs, and it's not a warbly-pretty laugh either, like Cinderella's birds. She actually snorts, and the space holding us apart gives a little. "Your mom was very . . ." She pauses, and I can't even imagine what she is going to say. "She was very insistent on how things should be."

My shoulders relax by about one centimeter, and I nod

in agreement. "She hasn't changed," I say. "She wants what she wants."

"Moms," Jessie says. The snort is gone, and Jessie looks perfect again, like a music box ballerina spinning, spinning, spinning.

She doesn't say anything, and I don't say anything, and it looks like maybe we've exhausted all the possible words, but then she says, "People believe a lot of weird crap. Like crystals and stuff. There's this girl at my studio who puts on copper ankle bracelets after we're done dancing. She thinks they will make her feet better."

I scratch the side of my head. "Don't you all have messed-up feet?"

We both look down at her flip-flops. Two toes are black under the nails. There are Band-Aids on four others. On one, I can see the blood seeping through. From the ankles down, she is a BodyBeautiful™ wasteland.

"These are in pretty good shape," she says, like we're talking about used cars or something. "Brianna thinks the copper will make her arches better. Also a bunch of BS, but dancers tend to be a superstitious lot."

I don't know what she means by arches but I'm seeing bridges and bodies and the curve of a whale breaking the surface of the sea. "Do you remember when we went to SeaWorld?" I blurt.

We are seven years old.
Our families go on vacation together.
We sit in the front row of the orca show and push our noses against the glass.
Turquoise water, leap and spray, our squeals, slickblackwhaleskin.

"Of course I do," she says. "We used to play whale and trainer."

My stomach churns. We took turns crouching on the edge of the pool and summoning the whale, who offered kisses. Instantly, heat courses through me. I'm sure I'm blushing at the thought of two girls kissing. Does Jessie remember that?

"It makes me sad now," says Jessie.

I can't look at her. I don't want to see her pity.

"The way they made them perform for us," she continues. "Whales shouldn't be in captivity like that."

"You mean you didn't mind?"

Confusion rolls across her face. "Mind what?"

"Nothing. Sorry." I don't like what she's doing to me. I'm a compass spinning, and I don't know which way to point.

Jessie fiddles with the strap of her bag. "I don't have a ton of time before I have to be back at the studio. Should we get lunch?"

I nod.

We order *khao man gai* from the Thai food cart. While we wait for the woman on the other side of the window to ladle broth into Styrofoam cups and lay strips of spiced chicken on a bed of rice, I notice a man in line for the vegan black bean bowls watching Jessie. He's older. Thirties maybe. A crisp white shirt stretches across his shoulders. When we pass him on the way to an empty table, his gaze sweeps across Jessie's ass. I want to slap him.

The edges are fraying.

I wanted Jessie, my Jessie.

I thought . . .

I hoped . . .

I don't fucking know what. That maybe seeing her would make me okay again. But this Jessie is such a . . . I don't know . . . such a girl. The kind of girl that men want and mothers want and photographers photograph. The kind that spins and dances, spotlighted from above.

Nothing like me.

JESSIE

Dawn doesn't look at me while we eat. She sits like a guy, thighs spread. The crotch of her sweatpants stretches between her legs. I half expect her to scratch her balls. I stare at her, trying to find the children we were.

She points to a man in a white shirt eating at a nearby table. "He wants to fuck you," she says.

He grins when I look over, rubbing one hand along the tight-shorn nape of his neck. A flush sweeps over me. Dawn notices and scowls. A woman walks by with three little shih tzus that start barking their heads off at Dawn.

"Little dogs are the worst," she says.

I can't keep up with this conversation. I'm already upset and she's erratic and it unsettles me. I have to admit to myself that I came here with a hope. A small stab of it in the ruin of my day. Maybe I would find my friend. The girl who was the sun around which I orbited. The hero of my made-up stories. That girl, that Dawn, was everything I'm not—outspoken, brash, brave. I thought, coming here, that maybe she could save me.

She growls in the back of her throat, and instantly I'm on alert.

"What's wrong with you?" The words are out of my mouth before I can stop them.

Dawn stares at me, and there is nothing recognizable in her eyes. My fork stops halfway to my mouth. This was a mistake.

"I need to get back to the studio," I stammer, reaching for my bag.

"Wait!" she says, grabbing my arm. Her grip is stronger than I expect. Another low guttural sound comes from her. It sends a shudder through me, and even in this crowded city block, I am afraid.

"We . . . can't . . . let . . ."

She forces each word out, and even though I'm scared, I lean in, needing to know what she is trying to say.

"Can't . . . let it . . . happen . . . to us."

She lets go of my arm and lowers her head. It swings back and forth, like a dog on the scent of a rabbit. Her breath comes rough and ragged, and her hands clench and unclench like she's in pain.

I can't move.

"Can't let what happen?" I whisper. "What's wrong?"

Her chest heaves, once, twice, again. When she meets my eyes, I can see she's regained some kind of control. "They caught the whale when she was a baby. Took her from the wild. Put her in a tank. Made. Her. Dance."

"It's okay," I murmur, because that's what you are supposed to say. "You're okay." Even though I'm sure that's not true. "We're okay." Because I want to believe.

Dawn clutches my hand, squeezing too tightly. "Do you know what happened?"

I shake my head, but before she can explain, there's a tense, coiled woman standing next to our table. No introductions necessary. I would know Dawn's mother anywhere. She is what they call *put together*.

"We should go," she says to Dawn.

Dawn shoots her a dark, hate-filled expression, but then she changes immediately. It's like Dawn has smacked against the hard wall of her mother and used the rebound to get control of herself.

"Everything is fine," she says, letting go of my hand. "Isn't it, Jessie?"

I look from one to the other. Between their two faces a whole story unfolds. I don't even have CliffsNotes.

"It's been a long time," I say, taking refuge in small talk.

Dawn's mother pastes a smile on her face. "Too long. It's good to see you." I only halfway believe this. "Your dad says that your ballet career is really taking off."

"Yeah," I say, "it's great."

The lie is like shooting myself in the head.

"What about school?"

I shrug. "I took the GED so I could dance full time."

She keeps smiling, but I see the flicker of her disapproval. So does Dawn. "The Ivy Leagues don't like GEDs, do they, Mother?"

It's a jab, but not at me.

"I'm not the Ivy League type," I say.

"Right," says Dawn. "You're the Sugar Plum Fairy type. The Ivy Leagues don't like head cases, either."

Her mother swoops in. "Well, I think it's wonderful that you're dancing, Jessie. And look at you! You're so thin! You're so beautiful! I wish Dawn had taken up ballet!"

I wince. Who says that kind of thing about their own daughter?

Dawn's face darkens. "Do you know what happened to the orca?"

I'm caught off guard again. "I have no idea."

"She went crazy. Attacked a trainer. Killed another one. Drowned him. Scalped him. Guarded his body."

The sunlight in Rose Square sours. The people nearest to us step away. Dawn's mother is about to blow a gasket. Dawn stands, pats her arm, patronizing. "Let's go, Mother." To me, she says, "Can you blame her? Can you blame the whale?"

I watch Dawn drag her mother toward the car. It resurrects the memory of the last time we were together. Our arms entwined. Our tears smeared on each other's faces. We were already blood sisters. We had pricked our fingers and pressed the pads together. Fingerprint on fingerprint. Blood to blood. A ritual. A kind of dance.

She's gone again.

The world feels cracked open and raw.

Like my feet.

As I'm leaving Rose Square, the man in the white shirt saunters toward me. "Hey," he says.

"Hey yourself."

Another time maybe, I would hold his gaze, let the edge of my lip curl upward, flirt. But I'm tired and I don't understand what just happened and Eduardo didn't pick me.

"Are you a dancer?" he asks.

"Yeah, I am," I say, surprised that he's noted the accoutrements—hair bun, ballet bag, leotard strap visible under my shirt—and drawn conclusions. But then I notice that he has a hard-on in his khaki trousers. It's not about the Sugar Plum Fairy. When he says *dancer* he doesn't mean ballet.

I skip the afternoon pointe class for the first time since I've been at Ballet des Arts. When I leave Rose Square, I ride the MAX train home and crawl into bed even though it's only three o'clock. I'm almost asleep when Dawn texts.

Don't be afraid of me.

My fingers tighten around the phone. I'm wide awake. The day twists into sharp focus. She did scare me and that makes me hate myself a little. Seeing Dawn was . . . What? Complicated, I guess. Like at the core she was familiar, but the outside was all different. Or maybe the other way around. Maybe she is a new person wrapped in the cloak of the old. I don't know.

Should I be? I ask.

No? Maybe? I don't know.

Wild suspicions fill me. Like maybe she's on drugs or being abused. Maybe the whole weird lunch was a cry for help.

Why was your mom there?

They don't let me drive.

???

It's hard to explain.

I'm lost. Maybe Dawn's mom is some kind of killer fembot. Now that I think of it, maybe my mom is one too. I hear Tamar in my head, counting out a four beat intro. Eduardo did not pick me. After the spring showcase, my mom will get her way after all. I'll be doing something practical: dental hygienist, medical technician, bookkeeper.

Are you okay? I text.

Can you clarify the question?

I want to write: *Are there fembots?* Instead I say, Is anyone hurting you?

Why would you ask that?

I don't know.

No one is hurting me.
My dad said you were sick.
It's complicated.
Is it cancer?
That, my friend, would be a piece of cake.
Then what?

She doesn't answer in words. She sends a picture of a page of notes. It's a careful list of dates and times and places. Mastiff. Meth house. Rape test. A record of what she calls fugues, whatever those are.

DAWN

The orca is still alive.

Off exhibit, of course. Can't risk another death. She's in a tank so small she can barely turn around. They feed her frozen fish and keep their distance, the keepers that made her murderous. It's 10:05, and I imagine that I understand the orca, circling, circling, circling, the way I pace this room. Ten steps to the window. Outside, the streetlights glow orange. Ten steps back to the door. Locked, from the inside at least. Five to my desk. The numbers on the clock radio are blue-green. I have a stack of scientific papers to read for class, but I can't settle. Sitting still makes me want to claw my eyes out. Or someone else's.

When we were girls, Jessie and I loved the orca show.

But it wasn't what it seemed, and neither is Jessie.

Jessie now, I mean. My mother is head-over-heels. All the way home . . . Jessie this, Jessie that. She wants to see her dance, promised we'd attend the spring showcase, whatever that is. How very mother-daughter-y of us, to go to the ballet together, to drown ourselves in a sea of tulle and satin.

Jessie now is:
poised, my mother's word

contained, silk-bound and trussed
so beautiful she makes my chest hurt

I start throwing shit out of my closet. Lacrosse stick from seventh grade. A winter coat. Sneakers, combat boots, jeans with holes, jeans without holes, a tweedy suit coat with a red-eyed kraken embroidered on the back. Roller skates.

The box is at the bottom.

I sit on the floor with it in my lap. The pink construction paper glued to it is peeling off. Third-grade Valentine's Day is ancient history. I've long since dumped the obligatory valentines, the ones I received only because the teacher said you couldn't leave anyone out.

Jessie and I decorated this shoebox together, and when we moved, I put all the bits of her I had inside of it. Opening the lid completely breaks the calendar. The spacetime continuum goes to hell. It's not today.

The smell of sage swallows me—velvetsmooth, silvershine. Pungent leaves we collected on a camping trip. Torn tickets from the time we saw the *Nutcracker* together. I liked the rats. Jessie decided to take ballet. There's a yellow plastic ring from a vending machine at the state fair where baby goats nibbled the tips of our fingers. Jessie's school pictures—kindergarten through fourth grade. In the last one, she has her hair in two braids. On the back, she wrote *Luv ya!* with a purple pen. Now she is all swanneck and liquid limbs and unfathomable. Too close to BodyBeautiful™ for me to swallow.

I replace the contents of the box and go back to pacing, torn between wanting to throw it away and clutching it to my chest. Jessie now isn't Jessie then. I want, I want, I want to peel back her skin and see my friend, the girl I knew.

And more than that—
I want her to see me.
The girl I am.

Downstairs, I hear the dishwasher start. My mother, my jailor, is awake, a rattle of keys at her waist. It's almost midnight. I crack the door. She is on the phone, excavating the countertop while she talks. Tap, tap, tap.

I go halfway down the stairs where I can listen because I know this is my dad in Alaska. They always talk late after his wife is asleep. She suffers from un-Christian jealousy. David is watching a late night TV show. Like I said, he doesn't have a confidence problem.

"We've ruled out Lyme disease and Creutzfeldt-Jakob," she says.

Creutzfeldt-Jakob. A mouthful of cumbersome syllables. Mad cow disease. That's what it means, but I have not ingested the brains of infected cattle. At least, I don't think I have, but I might if offered some.

"It's not epilepsy," she explains, obviously annoyed with my paternal unit on the other end of the line. "Definitively ruled out by the neurologist." She listens to whatever he is saying, tap, tap, tap. "You don't understand, Lars. She scares me. You should hear the sounds that come from her room. It's like there's an animal in there." Pause, tap, tap. "If we don't have a diagnosis, we can't fix her."

Fix her, fix her, fix her. There's a roaring in my ears. Patch-up, set right, repair, to take that which is broken and restore to its previous function. Fix. I raise my hands in front of my face. I test the joints. Each finger functions, a coordination of bones and sinew, muscle and nerve.

They work.

I function.

But . . .

. . . not to specifications, not the daughter they intended.

And this hurts so much more than I want it to, an agony-skewer that pins me to the stairs. Jessie asked if I had cancer. My mother would prefer that. Cancer is a bravery test that everyone understands. What I have no one understands, and it can't be cut out of me.

My mother interrupts a monologue on the other end of the line. "Before you go getting all high and mighty, you could consider picking up some of the slack."

That's me.

The slack.

"Take her up there with you this summer. Maybe the fresh air will do her good." She listens longer. He is probably suggesting prayer, his universal antidote to disappointment and trouble. "I can't believe you would even say that," she hisses into the phone. My head jerks up out of my hands. His religious persuasions rarely induce that kind of response.

My mother says, "She would never hurt the children. Never!"

The hard surface under me has vanished, and I'm falling, falling, falling into space, into dark, into the place where my father thinks I am capable of violence. The orca tank. Death row. Too far gone even for prayer.

Alaska. Summer. I am twelve. No wind. Stickyheat. A day when everyone and everything is pissed-off and redmad because Alaskans don't understand temperatures above sixty-five degrees. They've got me in the garden, picking caterpillars off the broccoli while my dad's new children memorize Bible verses.

There is no respite from the mosquitoes, a cloudarmy, buzzing, droning. They are hungry for blood. I peel my sleeve up and hold out my arm. I let one feed and watch her abdomen bloat.

Hold steady.

Drink deep.

Making a fist, flexing the muscles of my forearm, and watching the beast explode in a shower of fine, red mist.

My period comes for the first time. I hold my underwear out to my father. He turns away from the evidence of my womanhood and calls my pregnant stepmother to deal with such sudden and horrifying fecundity. A bear comes to eat raspberries behind the house. My father shoots his shotgun in the air to scare her off. He jokes about scaring off boys the same way. Boys that will want to fuck me.

As if I would want to fuck them.

When I go outside with blood running down my legs, the bear is there, ignoring my father, claiming space.

"Do what you have to do," my mother snaps before ending the call.

I hear her mutter under her breath. Something about good riddance and screw you and I hear her open a bottle of wine. She pours and drinks and cries.

We are nine.

We are in the closet in my room, which is very big and I have it rigged up like a fort with a beanbag chair and these little strings of twinkly lights and rows of books and my Ninja Turtle radio.

Like I said, we are in the closet.

I do not realize the irony of this because I am nine and I don't know about closets and I think rainbows are pretty because—duh—rainbows!

This is the game we play, Jessie and me, while all of our parents drink wine downstairs and make dinner together and listen to music. We pull down our underwear. Jessie's are always bright colors. Mine are always white. We put marbles in between the lips of our vulvas and pull up our underwear and dance to music on the Ninja Turtle radio.

This feels nice.

It makes the dancing fun.

Even then Jessie is doing ballet, but she's just started and still stumps and flops around like me. We are not different then. Not like we are now. Longlean versus shortstout. Freegrace versus stucksolid.

We're the same.

We like the way the marbles feel.

When I'm tired of dancing, I flop on the beanbag chair and pull my pants and underwear down a few inches. I'm not all the way naked or anything, but I'm exposed from hip bones to the round lump of my pelvis.

I close my eyes.

This is key.

Jessie has stopped dancing. She sneakcreeps closer. Her warmth oozes along the left side of me, the bared hip. She's going to touch me. I know that much. But I don't know when because of the eyes being closed. The key.

I want to open my eyes but that will wreck everything. We have perfected this and part of perfection is the unbearable, closed-eye waitingwaitingwaiting.

Her touch, when it arrives after forever, is deft. A single swipe of an index finger across the top of my pubic mound. It sends a tremor through me. It's like the weightless moment when you jump in an elevator at just the right time.

I sit up laughing, breathless.

"My turn," she says.

And it is.

For us—at nine—this is our game. It must be played together. You can't be temporarily weightless alone. I try when Jessie can't come over. I lie in the closet on the beanbag and close my eyes, but no matter how I swirl my hand in the air above me, I can't fool myself. I always know when my finger will touch flesh, and it's not the same as when Jessie touches me.

And although we don't feel bad and can't believe we are bad, we know better than to tell anyone about our game or the marbles.

It's my dad who catches us, when I'm leaning over Jessie and it's her turn.

"What the—?" he says.

His face goes blotchy.

He jerks me up by the arm, smacks my bottom, and tells me to sit on my bed.

Jessie cries and gets yelled at too.

After that, the closet is off-limits.

My dad catches my mother kissing Jessie's father—more than kissing, fucking—and we move away from home, away from Jessie. A fresh start in a new place. But the shiny edges wear off within a year. David sniffs around my mother. She sniffs back. The fresh start is declared a failure. Dad moves to Alaska. We move again to this shit golf course in this shit suburb of Portland. Another new school for me.

David sticks.

Like gristle in my throat.

When I can't listen to my mother crying anymore, I heave my body off the stairs and back to my room, the four walls, the tightness of it. There's an e-mail from my dad, the man who doesn't want me. A helpful missive: *We are praying for you.*

JESSIE

The next morning I skip class again. What's the point? I lie in bed, watching dust motes float in the bits of sun that poke through along the edges of the blinds. I try to read one of Ed's books. It's about some macho army guy hunting down gun traffickers in Mali. Five pages in, I toss the paperback across the room. Who cares?

When Patrice knocks, I tell her I'm sick.

Mom calls and I don't answer.

Nita texts. Where the hell are you? Tamar is going to blow a gasket.

When I don't answer, she says, Rehearsals start this afternoon.

Which is exactly why I'm not at the studio.

You will ruin everything for the rest of us.

I didn't think ballet was a team sport.

Screw you.

I am a bird hit by a car. My wings are splayed on the pavement. My legs go in the wrong directions. Drops of blood spot the edges of my beak. The final performance of the year is supposed to be celebratory, but this feels more like a firing squad.

Eduardo did not pick me.

Another call from my mother followed by a text. Are you avoiding my calls?

To my mother, ballet has always been an extracurricular, a creative outlet, a way to stay in shape. She believes a girl becoming a woman needs to be practical. She says *Ballet is no way to support yourself.* She says *Don't expect a man to take care of you.* She says *Your only viable option is school.*

But I need the control and the perfection of motion.

I crave the way my body masters the dance.

Without it, I am lost.

YOU NEED TO CHECK IN NOW OR I AM DRIVING DOWN THERE.

I throw the phone across the room and hear the screen crack and I don't even care. It's not like I have a million friends or a boyfriend wanting to hang out all the time. I don't have anything but ballet.

Patrice knocks again. "Are you awake?"

I don't answer.

The door cracks. She peeks in and catches my eyes open. "How are you feeling?"

"Like crap."

She gives me a sympathetic look and sits on the edge of the bed. "What's wrong? Stomach ache? Cramps? Is it that time of the month?" Patrice pats me on the shoulder.

"Nothing like that. Yesterday was rough."

She nods like she gets it even though she can't possibly.

"Here's the deal," she says. "I try to give you your space as much as possible, but you have got to call your mom. Otherwise you're going to get me in big trouble."

I glance toward my phone in the corner of the room.

She sees where I'm looking and retrieves it with a raised eyebrow. It still works even though the screen is shot. "Promise?" she asks, holding out the phone.

I take it and promise even though this totally sucks.

As soon as the door shuts, I dial the home number, hoping for voice mail.

It's Dad. "Everything all right?"

I tense up immediately. "Why wouldn't it be?"

"Just a question."

"I'm not dying or anything."

"Well, that's good to hear." His voice is stone flat, and it totally rubs me the wrong way.

"Why doesn't anyone in this family ever react to anything?"

He hesitates, proving my point.

"See!"

"Jessie," he says, "would you like to talk to your mom?"

"No," I say, without bothering to keep the irritation out of my voice.

"Mom wants to talk to you."

"I gathered that from all her messages."

He must put the phone to his chest because I hear his muffled call to my mother, and then he's back at full volume, saying, "Hold on a minute."

"I talked to Dawn," I say. "I saw her."

There is a long pause.

"Is she as much of a mess as her mom said she was?"

It's like a wildfire explodes inside of me. "How can you say that?" I hiss. "You don't even know her."

He tries to placate me. "Monica said she had a lot of problems."

"It's totally her mom's fault," I snap even while I know that

I don't have an actual clue what Dawn's problems are.

"Blame the parents," my dad says. "Tried and true teenager tactic. Mom's right here. She wants to talk to you about the end of the program. Love you. Bye."

And he's gone as easy as handing off the phone.

"Hi, honey. Patrice said you weren't feeling well. What's up?"

"I'm fine."

"If you're fine, why aren't you in class?"

"Why do you care?"

She exhales loudly, probably Zen-breathing herself to another cosmic plane. One with a more acceptable daughter. "Your dad and I have been talking about when you are moving home."

"I'm not."

"Honey—"

I head her off. "Which show do you want me to get you tickets for?"

I'm out of bed with the phone mashed to my ear, throwing things in my dance bag. It's not too late for me to make it to pointe class.

"We need to . . ."

What I need is to get to rehearsal. I have a show to prepare for, and even if it's not Eduardo's piece, there's no freaking way I'm going to prove my mother right. "The tickets are selling out really fast," I lie. "And I can only get comp tickets for one show. Which weekend are you coming? Matinee? Evening?"

She sighs, and I know exactly what her face looks like. It's a grimace she saves for big credit card bills and broken appliances. "Opening night, please."

"Two tickets, opening night. Check. I've got to run now."

"Jessie," she says, "Dad will be back a few days after the show closes to help you pack up and drive home."

I clutch my pointe shoes to my chest. "You don't need to pack me up. I'm staying."

"The program ends after the showcase."

"I might be asked to stay on."

"How many of you girls are there? Thirteen? Fourteen? I'm just trying to manage your expectations, Jessie. This isn't the only thing you're good at."

If there are other things I'm good at, I don't know what the fuck they are. I want to throw the phone again, and this time, do a better job of destruction.

My mother breaks the silence. "Ed and Patrice's son will be home from college for the summer in mid-June. He'll need his room back." She tries to sound motherly. "Your dad and I are really looking forward to your performance."

"Bullshit," I snap. "You want me to quit."

Her voice stretches very thin. "Your dad and I believe that if it doesn't work out for you in Portland, then it wasn't meant to be. We'll see you at the performance."

She ends the call before I can, and rage is what propels me back to the studio.

They can't take this from me.

I won't let them.

When I finally get to the studio, Eduardo's rehearsal is still in progress.

"Look who finally decided to show up." Nita scowls at me from the couch in the foyer.

I ignore her and stand at the viewing windows to watch. *Four Variations* is a lyrical, delicate piece that will feature Lily and Caden in the pas de deux. Brianna and the others will be the corps de ballet. The lilting music carries each dancer across the floor.

Even at this early stage in rehearsals, I can tell Lily will be exquisite. Her beauty is an ache in my chest, an echo of how I felt watching Selene. I hold on to that wanting and it swirls together with the anger still seething in my belly. If this is the life I want, I have to take it, and if that means dancing for Vadim, that is what I'm going to do.

A few moments later, Vadim arrives. Lily is mid-arabesque when he strides into the studio and changes the music. German techno synth blasts through the speakers. Eduardo glares at him. Vadim smiles a honey-covered grin and taps his watch with one finger. Eduardo throws up his hands and waves Lily and the rest of the dancers out of the studio.

"I can't believe Vadim is provoking him like that," says Mimi, joining me and Nita in the foyer. "Does he want to lose his company spot? That's what everyone thinks is going to happen."

The irony does not escapes me. Vadim is throwing away the thing the rest of us so desperately want. But he's a man. Half the companies in the country would spit blood to have him in their top spot. We girls are disposable.

As soon as the others have cleared out, Vadim waves us into the center of the studio and shuts the door to the foyer. He walks around us, muttering under his breath in Russian. On the second circuit he crouches before me, staring up the length of my body, assessing the view from below. He does the same to Nita. For Mimi, he drags the piano bench over and stands on it, looking down at her.

"We are building something new," Vadim announces, his accent oozing a stew of Slavic creative juices. He slaps his hand on top of the piano. Good thing Franz is done for the day. No one messes with his piano. "For this piece," Vadim says, "I ask you to dig inside. We are going to carve space and sculpt new shapes with our bodies." The timbre of his voice lengthens, deepens, and burns with intensity. "Ugly. Lustful. Lonely. It is all one. Together we will birth the world."

Nita catches my eye. She looks as worried as I feel. Mimi's arms are wrapped double around her rib cage. Her lips are pursed so tightly that they look sewn. I want to offer her nail scissors to snip the threads, but I feel the same nervousness about what's coming.

He waves us toward the barre. "Warm up however you like."

Mimi begins a series of deep pliés in second position facing the barre.

Nita and I help each other stretch, sitting face to face with our legs straddled and our feet pressed together. She leans back, and I am pulled toward her until my chest is flat on the floor and my head is on her stomach. When the pull in my inner thighs has dulled to a steady ache, I lean back and pull her forward.

At least this is familiar, a small comfort.

Mimi is trying to do Tamar's pointe class standards to nightclub music and is getting more and more flustered. For her, losing the company spot means having to move back to France. Nita and I do crunches and then stand for a few minutes of fast footwork at the barre. By the time we return to the center of the studio, Vadim is pacing. He has stripped off his street clothes and waits for us in a white T-shirt and black tights. His body is all sharp planes and cut muscles—a man's body.

He begins to dance. There's an animalistic quality to the way he moves. Not anything that resembles ballet. It's strange and threatening. The three of us exchange glances. We don't know what to make of the movements or that he seems oblivious to our presence. I can read the tension in the other girls. It matches my own. The anger that drove me to the studio has dissipated, and I'm starting to think this was a terrible idea.

My temples throb and my joints ache. I roll my shoulders forward and backward. I send my left leg into loose rotations. Everything lengthens, and I imagine stretching out to all corners of the room. This, at least, feels good.

Suddenly Vadim is behind me, his hands on my hips. "Do that again."

I feel the warmth of him through the thin fabric of my leotard. My face is framed against the white T-shirt he is wearing. "Swing your leg. Loose like that," he says. "And when I take you off balance, rise en pointe."

I toss my left leg high in front, toes pointed, knee bent akimbo. The ball of my femur turns slick as oil in the hip socket. When it reaches the side, Vadim's hands tilt my entire body to the right. I rise on point which unbalances me further. My back presses against his chest, and to keep my balance, I instinctively bend my leg and wrap it behind him. My calf cups his ass. The shape we make in the space is angry and all sharp edges.

"Arms wide. Not like that!" he says, when my limbs assume the smooth, rounded lines that Tamar demands. "Tight. Stiff. Flat. Like you will not let anyone pass."

I hesitate.

"Do it," he snaps, and my elbows lock into place. My fingers are blades. His left hand flattens against my abdomen. His fingers splay over me, grazing my pubic bone. A jolt of arousal explodes at his touch. Vertigo sweeps over me. I remember.

I remember. I remember. Dawn and I used to play a game like this. They found us. They caught us. They told us that only bad girls did things like that. My throat is swelling shut. I want to get out of here. I'm sure I'm going to fall. The studio is distorting, twisting. My reflection in the mirror is monstrous.

I break away from Vadim in a panic, gulping for air.

He seizes my arm, hard enough for me to cry out. The force of it whips me back toward him, and he grabs my shoulders, hauling me en pointe. We're eye-to-eye, and his face is fierce.

I think he holds me there forever.

His chest rises and falls in great heaves.

He's a tidal wave taking me under.

And then . . .

Vadim releases me. His expression warms. He pats me on the ass. "Well done, love." I drop my head between my knees, trying not to pass out. I feel like I've left my body. This isn't dance. I'm not supposed to be this out of control.

When I look up, Nita and Mimi are staring at me like deer in headlights.

He is going to eat us alive.

Vadim rubs his hands together like he is anticipating the meal. "This is how we will work. Try things. Experiment. Take risks. Can you do this?"

None of us say anything.

"Can you?!" he demands.

Nita crosses her arms over her chest and nods curtly at him. "Good."

A puff of protest escapes Mimi.

He wheels on her. "Do you have a problem?"

"It's not even ballet," she says.

"No?" Vadim walks away even as she tries to respond. "And what is ballet to you?" He is at the stereo cuing up new music.

"It's steps with names. It's beautiful. It's perfect."

He scoffs at her. "Try being not-perfect. It's far more interesting."

Vadim turns to me. "I like the way you move."

"I . . . uh . . ." My breath comes in shallow pants. I don't know what I'm trying to say.

Vadim's eyes narrow. "Spit it out. You're not a child."

I force myself to stand tall, almost as tall as he is. I find the one description that comes close. "It feels dangerous," I say.

"Good," he says, practically licking his lips. "Then we are on the right track."

DAWN

From: Dr. Stephen Kerns

To: Class Roster, OB-012 Advanced Topics in Animal Behavior

RE: Ethology Assignment

Good morning!

Our last discussion was excellent. Great participation, people. We've got another online session coming up in a few days. Topic: evolution via natural selection with an emphasis on animal behavior. You can download the background readings from the course home page. Make sure you read up. Our discussions are your chance to get your questions answered and for me to assess your understanding of the material.

Today I posted a hands-on assignment. You have two weeks to complete it. The task is to create a methodology for collecting behavioral data and then use that methodology as a basis for observation of and data collection on actual animals. (This does not mean your dog, people!)

My rationale: It's one thing to get theoretical. It's quite another to understand the amount of time, work, and effort necessary to collect sufficient reliable data on animal behavior. Get started soon. You can pretty much expect things to go wrong. Animals are unpredictable.

Best,
Dr. Kerns

I get to work right away. Ethology is the science of animal behavior. Lab coats perching over mice in a maze. People with binoculars reading leg bands on birds. Jane Goodall sitting in the jungle with a clipboard in her hand. Someone is always watching. The word comes from the Greek *ethos*, meaning nature or disposition. What is one's true nature? How do we dispose of the body?

I read further because this is what I do. I analyze. I study. I observe.

Ethology is also the study of human behavior and social organization from a biological perspective. In a broader context, ethos describes the customs of a species, a group, a people. A person? I look around my room.

I observe:
hole in the drywall, result of aggressive behavior
dirty clothes mounded high, poor attention to personal grooming
the window, an escape route

A sudden wave of nausea hits me. My head spins from the break in logic. I am watching myself watch myself. Scientists talk about the observer effect: the way the act of watching and measuring changes that which is being observed. Perhaps I am not an ideal subject for this assignment.

I'm twelve and my boobs grow into fleshy, pneumatic globs. I shove the unwelcome growths into a sports bra and hide them under sweaters. Not that it helps. In grocery stores, at the bus stop, on the way home from the library—leers, looks, gropes, grabs. Constant observation. I'm under glass. I'm underfoot. I'm fair game.

Walking home from school—a copper flash. A coin on the sidewalk. I'm crouching to retrieve it when the man at the bus stop grabs his crotch and says, "I see you'll go down for a penny."

Deciding between Heath bars and Butterfingers in a convenience store—a man lurching. He palms my breast in a big meaty hand, squeezes hard enough to hurt. Then he is paying for a tallboy of Busch like nothing happened.

My mother catching me walking home alone at night—think of what could happen. Anyone could do anything. The things men do.

The observer effect is:
I do not pick up change on the ground
I do not eat Heath bar or Butterfinger
the night is not mine

I download Dr. Kerns's assignment and print it out. He suggests watching squirrels in the park or birds at a feeder or an animal at the zoo. All of which seem freaking lame. Squirrels are big-tailed rats, and house finches at a pile of seed aren't much better.

I decide to observe the bear.

Somewhere in the back of my mind, as long as I've been lucid, lurks the awareness of the bear. Ever since I stumbled upon her in Hobart's backyard, she's been a scent in my nose, the kind that you notice at first but then become used to—wet dog, garbage gone bad, burned toast.

A bear.

I grab my journal and a pencil and tuck my digital camera into the front pocket of my flannel shirt.

David is at work, and my mother is at the salon getting her highlights retouched or her ladyparts waxed so I don't need to climb out of the window this time. I take the stairs at a run, excited by the prospect of seeing the bear again. I'm halfway across the wheat field when a thought hits me. Will she make me go dark?

My feet stutter to a stop in the soft earth.

I close my eyes. Self-imposed darkness.

It's midmorning. Cloudy but not raining. Yet. My ears detect the distant rumble of the highway, but the streets here are quiet. Parents at work. Children at school. Old people still coaxing their limbs to move. I have to think about things like that now. About limbs and whether they will work or not. Old woman thoughts. Sick woman thoughts.

I keep listening, blind-eyed, for the huff and rustle of the bear, the scritch of her claws. There is something about her that is connected to the fugues, but I don't know what it is.

My skin tingles.

Will my body let me down?

Is that even the right question?

Suddenly, I am of two minds again. Both watcher and the watched. I am afraid to go dark, but I also want to know what happens there. Heartpound, thrillseek, the zingzap, heartstop of a high place, a fast descent, falling.

My eyes snap open.

Blue light over the wheat field. The new plants seem to grow before my eyes. The soil twitches with roots, seeking-sucking, branchingtwining. My mother, the doctors, my father, the stepfather—they think I am breaking down, but this heightened awareness does not feel like a malady.

What if it is not affliction?

What if I am something new?

This is an important thought. I scribble it down in the journal. I write: must make more observations, test the theory. And then I put the journal away and head into the forest toward the bear.

The last time I was here I wasn't thinking too clearly. It takes me nearly an hour of wandering to find the chain-link fencing around Hobart's property. How the hell did I get in there? Vague images resurface—rusted fencing, a gap, crawling through dirt. I walk the perimeter looking for an access point. As I'm crossing in front of the single wide trailer, the door bangs open and the dog named Bitch bounds out.

She sees me, barks once, urinates in a patch of weeds, and approaches.

I'm scratching her head through the narrow opening between gate and fence when Hobart comes out of the trailer.

He stands on the step, rubbing his eyes.

"You again?" he says.

When I don't respond, he stumps down the steps and up the driveway toward me.

The dog licks my hand and whines.

"What do you think you're doing?" He glares at me with bloodshot, watery eyes. "I thought I told you to stay the fuck away from here."

"I want to see the bear again."

"Oh you do, do you?" A phlegm-filled rumble spills from his mouth. Maybe it's supposed to be a laugh. Or he's got emphysema. He makes a move as if he is going to open the gate. "Come in. I'll get you a beer while you have a look around."

"I don't drink," I say, looking up from the dog.

"I don't drink," he simpers. "Dumb ass. Maybe you should." He grabs the dog by her choke collar and pulls her away from the gate. "Get out of here."

"Look," I say, "I've got an assignment for school."

Under a sheen of sweat, his neck is red and ropey, and I smell the stink of him. "Last time you was here, you threatened to call the cops on me and now you want to come for a goddamn field trip. You got big balls, don't you?"

I pull the camera out of my pocket—an innocent prop. "I just want to watch the bear for a while. Take a few pictures."

Hobart looks like he is going to pop a vein. "You're pulling some PETA shit, aren't you? One of them ecoterrorist types."

People for the Ethical Treatment of Animals. They're the ones that set fire to research labs and throw pig's blood on women in fur coats. I can see the appeal.

The dog sidles back to the fence, closer to me.

Hobart glowers, his face a landscape of hard times. "I don't know how you got inside last time, but if you come on my property again, you won't be walking off of it. If you get me."

I remember the sign I saw last time—*You're In My Sights.* He doesn't have to spell it out.

The dog licks my hand, and Hobart explodes.

He hauls off and hits the dog across the muzzle. She yelps, a horrible, pain-filled dogshriek, and I'm against the fence, flailing to get at him. He smacks her again, and she slinks low, whining, and I'm yelling obscenities at him, and if words were bullets, he'd be riddled with them, bleeding out in the gravel.

He spits at my feet, a brown-tinged mucus splat, grabs the dog by the collar, and drags her back to the trailer. I rattle the gate with all my strength, willing the rusty piece of shit to crumple.

It doesn't.

He stops at the door and turns back toward me, wearing a hateface. "My dog. My bear. I'm in my rights. This ain't fucking Zanesville. Now git out of here before I blow your fucking head off."

Zanesville?

The door slams behind him.

I collapse against the gate, breathing hard.

I don't know how long I stay here.

Long enough for it to start raining.

Long enough for it to get dark.

Long enough for my stepfather to get home before I do.

A tactical error.

Another miscalculation.

He pours scotch over ice, pulls off the noose of his tie, and unbuttons the white collar of his dress shirt. I don't want to see him or smell him. I hope he gets cirrhosis of the liver. David takes up too much space in the kitchen, in my house, in my mother, which is disgusting.

"Where have you been?" he asks, draining his glass.

I already want to fight. "Where's my mother?"

He eyes me. "She'll be home late. She's doing a presentation at the health club. Your mom's a go-getter."

"Fetch," I say under my breath.

The capillaries in his face dilate. He reddens. "What did you say?"

I mime throwing a ball for a dog. "You said she's a go-getter.

I said fetch." I open the fridge, deliberately turning my back on him, a risky move. My hand reaches for a Coke. The rest of me is antenna-tuned on the body behind me, its bulk, its smell.

I hear another pour of scotch.

"Your mother works hard. I work hard. We put a roof over your head. Buy your clothes." He eyeballs me when I face him. Doesn't hide his disgust. "You have no respect for anything. Look at yourself. Can't you even shower? And no respect for us. For your mom. She gave up everything for you."

The lie rubs me the wrong way.

"For me?" I demand. "For me?"

He shrugs me off.

"She didn't give. She took." I speak carefully. He should hear me. "My mother took everything from me so she could fuck you and my friend's dad and whoever else wanted her to spread her waxed legs." The words rip their way out. My vision flickers, shorts out. For a split second I'm blind, then everything has a steel-blue sheen and David is looming over me.

His fists are balled at his side. "You self-absorbed little shit. After all we've put up with . . ."

I lean toward him. I want him to hit me. I want a reason.

But he leans away, unclenches his hands, controls himself, speaks with gravel in his voice. "You have until September. College or a job or you can go lie in a ditch for all I care, but one way or another, you are out of this house by fall." There's spittle at the corners of his mouth. "Everyone has to make their own life. Your mother chose me. You need to figure some shit out."

He doesn't hit me.

Instead, he picks up his scotch and his keys and his briefcase, and he goes upstairs into the bedroom he shares with my mother. Through the rushing in my ears, I hear the TV come on. I turn in a slow circle, trying to remember where I am and how to get out of here. Through the aqueous light, I read the signs on the wall. *Change begins one step at a time. A better you, a beautiful you. Start fresh today.*

My mouth is full of too-sharp teeth. My gums are bleeding. Seismic tremors shake my body. I look at my forearms and see the musculature writhing under the skin.

I run up the stairs.

My room.

The door.

I lock it, hoping that is enough.

Nightdark.

Naked. Fleshthrash. Legs tangled in sheets. Breathepant, pantbreathe. Hands ache.

Wallscrush—outoutoutoutoutout.

Brainsieve. Blankhead. Emptymind.

There is a sound—resonant, sharp, bone on wood. It repeats. Twitch toward the knocking.

Dawn?

That voice. Mother. Recognize the careful container of cautious words.

Dawn?

I am coming back now. To my mother, at the door, on edge, in a fix—I respond in a low growl. Smell her perfume and the lacquer on her fingernails and the faint hint of beeswax and say enough to keep her from coming through the door with her toothpick lockpick.

Bees take me to summer and humbuzzswarm. The sweetness of honey on my lips takes me back to Jessie.

I unclench my fists.

JessieJessieJessie.

I cannot hate everything about my mother because she brought Jessie back to me.

In fits and starts, the pieces of today revive.

These are data.

There is a pattern.

Whatever is happening to me is not random. Understand and I could stop it. Understand and I could control it. I write in the journal even though it hurts my hands to hold a pen. *Anger spawned this fugue.*

JESSIE

"You have to unlearn everything," Vadim snaps, correcting me again for being too classical. His choreography twists ballet into new shapes with no names. It's an ugly, fractured dance. I can't stand the way we look in the mirror.

"You start like this." His feet are parallel—ballet's sixth position. He rises on his toes, bends his knees, curves his body, and drops his head toward the floor. It is a posture full of yearning. "Understand?" he asks. I nod and take his place. I'm precarious, curled like this en pointe.

He moves in close. His body becomes a hard plane that supports me. He slides his arm under my breasts. I tense at his touch.

"Let your head fall right like the neck is broken."

My nose jams against his bicep. I smell his sweat, tangy and crisp. At the edge of his sleeve, I see the trailing ink of a tattoo.

"When I lift you, curl up more tightly. Knees to chest. Fetal."

The synth music pounds through me. My calves burn, and I doubt I can stand from this position.

Then I'm not standing.

I'm floating, cupped in Vadim's arms, nestled against his chest.

It's a moment of standstill, of expectation.

"Put your arms around my neck," he rasps. "Interlace your fingers."

When I do, my body twists to face him and my legs, still folded to my chest, spread until I'm straddled across his belly. Vadim's arms support my thighs. Our bodies press together. His chest rises and falls. The deep beat of the music reverberates through us, and I'm suddenly aroused, wet between the legs and shuddering. He shifts his arms and slides me down his body until I'm in a misshapen arabesque with his crotch pressed against me.

"Better," he says, releasing me. "You felt something."

I meet his eyes, wondering if he knows what it was I felt.

His lip twitches upward.

And I know he knows.

I take a break while he works with Nita and Mimi. He is building the dance in short vignettes. Sometimes all four of us dance together. Other times in pairs. Sometimes alone. The relationships in the dance are constantly shifting.

This is what he wants to explore.

The ties that bind us. The ones that fray and break. Others that stretch but hold. He gives us homework. Write about jealousy. Think about longing. What are your desires? He expects my body to reveal what I have written.

He summons me back for the next vignette.

I flush when he says my name.

He directs Nita and Mimi where he wants them and takes his place at center stage. "You are here," he says, pointing directly in front of him. "Turn to me as if I can give you what you want."

When I do, he presses me against him and runs his palms

over the curve of my ass, crouching as he does until his face is at the level of my crotch and his hands are gripping the tops of my thighs.

"Lean back," he growls, his man smell rising.

I spread my arms wide and bend my upper back until it is arching toward the floor. He is slick with sweat, and I am ravenous for him. He moves his hand to the middle of my back and presses me upright. I fold into him, squeezing my abdomen and curling around his arm and shoulder. For one moment, I feel safe, a kitten in a cat's mouth, then he spins me away, and I'm facing Nita, hands together. We push against each other. We clasp hands and circle, faster and faster. Another reversal and we are pulling against one another, fighting over something we both want but only one can have.

Nita is fierce as she uses her body weight against me. Her eyes hold something close to hatred. I don't know why we are fighting. Why do we let him do this to us? A moment later I am broken arms and legs and grief and Mimi embraces me, each sweep of her arms a caress.

Thus it goes.

Under Vadim's command, we are lovers and murderers, friends and enemies. We twist through the contortions he demands. And there is so much longing. Never enough to fill the void.

"Repeat," he commands.

And we do.

Again and again, until I can taste the laundry soap he uses on his clothes.

Until his hands have traversed the length of me.

Until I will do anything he asks.

Until I realize that the opposite of longing is oblivion.

By the end of rehearsal, I feel raw and manhandled. I slump into the foyer, wishing I could teleport to my bed. The last thing I expect is to see Dawn slouching against the wall. Her jeans hang on her hips and her legs cross at the ankles. She's wearing a navy blue bowling shirt that says Ned and two-tone Doc Martins.

What's she doing here? Has she been waiting for me?

When she sees me she pulls her hands out of her pockets. Her smile is almost shy, an apology and a plea all at once. I remember our odd and uncomfortable lunch, the way it held a shadow of the friends we used to be.

She raises one hand in salute.

"Hi, Ned," I say.

Her grin broadens, and freckles hip-hop across her cheeks. I'm surprised how happy that makes me, especially after the last two hours.

"What are you doing here?"

She holds out one hand, palm up.

There's a flash of yellow.

It's a cheap plastic ring with a split in the back so it can fit any finger. I pick it up and my heart skitters. The ring has a bumblebee on it with a round, striped body and a cute, smiley face.

I know this ring. It's an artifact.

"I can't believe it," I say. "It's from the fair."

"Yeah," she says, almost shy.

The ring is like a spark, a miniature sun in the hollow of my chest. The great, swallowing emptiness that engulfed me during rehearsal suddenly has a point of light in it. We are not bad girls. We are not bad.

I can barely speak. "You kept it."

She nods.

"That was so long ago," I say, as the memories are resurrected by a piece of plastic made in China. The goats nibbled our fingers. The waiting room of Ballet des Arts seems to wobble on its foundation.

The other girls are leaving. Mimi brushes past without a word. Nita says, "See you tomorrow."

Vadim flicks off the lights in the studio. "I need to lock up," he says, glancing from Dawn to me and back again, dissecting what is between us.

"I need to change my shoes," I say. "I'll be fast."

He nods and heads to the men's changing room to retrieve his things.

I sit on the floor and untie the ribbons knotted at my ankles. When I pull off the pointe shoes and roll the tights up, Dawn gets an eyeful of my battered feet.

"Don't show those to my mother," she says. "It will ruin her good impression of you."

I peer up at her. "What are you talking about?"

She waves her hand dismissively. "BodyBeautiful™. My mother's magical elixir. She likes how pink you are."

I make a face at her. "What's that supposed to mean?"

"Nothing."

"How did you find me?" I ask, still feeling a little shell-shocked by her sudden appearance in my ballet world.

"My mother picks the lock to my room, and now she's stalking you too, apparently. I stalked her back. Looked in her phone. Lots of Google searches on Jessie Vale."

I shove my pointe shoes in my bag and pull sweats on over my tights and leotard. "That's creepy."

"You're telling me?"

Vadim returns and gestures us toward the door, impatient. Selene must be waiting. "Who's your girlfriend?" he asks, with more accent than usual.

Something like a growl comes from Dawn. She tucks an arm around my waist. "I've known Jessie my whole life," she says as we follow him out.

"Ah," he purrs, "then you know how fascinating she can be." He locks the outer door to the studio. As he strides down the block, he calls over his shoulder, "Don't waste your energies, Jessie. I need you in the dance."

Dawn glares as he disappears around the corner. "Kind of possessive, isn't he?"

"And you're not?"

I meant it as a joke, but she lets go of me like I've slapped her, and even though her closeness was making me a little nervous, the sudden gulf between us is as cold as outer space. I've still got the bee ring clutched in one fist. I hold it out to her, a peace offering. "Do I get to keep it?"

She nods, appeased.

"Well?" I say, tilting my head toward the ring in my hand. "Do the honors?"

Her expression changes again. I've never known a face like hers, one that moods sweep across like spring weather. I remember this too, the way she couldn't hide anything. Was I ever like that? I don't remember. In my family, dissembling became a life skill.

She takes the ring and slides it on my finger, and the dark city seems to spin slowly around us. She breaks the spell with a jingle of keys. "Can you drive? I'm not supposed to."

I come back to myself, stiffen a little, uncomfortable again with the sudden closeness. I think of Vadim. He provokes me too, but not like this. His penetration is a challenge. Dawn's touch is a reminder of the things I've lost.

I take the keys. "If you don't drive, how'd you get here?"

"I drove," she says, back to brusque, the way she was when we met for lunch.

"Why aren't you supposed to?"

"Remember the not-cancer problem?"

I nod.

"That."

I stop her. "Please tell me what's going on." Dawn won't look at me. She is silent so long that I ask again. "Please."

"I have these . . . episodes. They're called fugues. Like blackouts, I guess. I do things, but I don't remember. That's why they don't want me to drive."

"What causes the blackouts?"

She shakes her head. "They don't know."

Dawn points to an SUV parked on the corner. I unlock the doors and open the back to throw my dance bag in. A cloud of perfumed air about chokes me. The backseat is full of makeup samples and a box of hot pink satin bags.

I start the car and roll down all the windows.

"It's my mother's car," says Dawn, holding her nose. "Forgive me."

"What's in the bags?"

"Napalm," she offers, deadpan. "Obliterates female flaws."

DAWN

I watch her drive.

She does not tap the steering wheel. Not once.

Jessie only holds on with one hand. A point on the wheel that sends us hurtling through the curves and up, up, uphill to the place I want to take her. She is wearing the ring. Everything about her sets me humming. Up, up, uphill to a park overlooking the city.

It's dark. The streetlights glow orange on the wet road. The park will close soon. We have to hurry for one last ride. When the glow of the carousel comes into view, her intake of breath is audible. A whisper, a memory, the past.

She parks so we can see it through the rain-spotted windshield. Clutches the steering wheel, leans forward. I drink her. Colorsoundscent. Everything is moving very fast. Too fast. The animals transform into a blur of colors. I sway in my seat. The music jangles, tinny and muted through the windshield.

"It's like the one we went to in Tacoma that time," she says, without looking away from the color and blur.

"It's the same one," I say.

She looks at me, raising an eyebrow. "That's impossible."

"They moved it here when they remodeled the zoo in Tacoma."

Her face bursts open like a night flower. "What are we waiting for?"

We race to the carousel like leaves flying. Uncatchable. The ride is ending, and a couple unglues themselves from a dragon. They've been kissing and wobble as they disembark, light-headed from lack of oxygen.

"Last ride," says the man selling tickets. "You're just in time."

This makes Jessie laughskipdance up the stairs to the platform. She trails her fingers along a gilded horse, a leaping zebra, a jeweled giraffe, and I follow the trail her touch leaves, breathing the smell of her, the sweet sweat, the wonder.

She chooses the wooden rabbit, draped in a garland of carved roses.

I ride the bear.

And we're spinningspinningspinning into space.

JESSIE

The stupid guy manning the carousel practically has to drag us off the ride.

"I can't believe it," I say, as we clang through the gate. "I thought I'd never see that rabbit again. It's my favorite." As soon as my feet hit the grass, I throw my arms wide and spin on my axis. I feel like a kid, and I don't ever want to stop spinning.

Eventually I get dizzy, and the rain is seeping through the shoulders of my hoodie. When I stop rotating, the ground does not cooperate, and I sway drunkenly. Dawn is next to me, stolid and earthbound.

We are, right now in this moment, like we were—two halves of one girl that fit together perfectly. I have been living severed all this time. My glued-up heart re-cracks.

"We lost so much," I say, when we are back in the car.

Dawn's shoulders curve inward, her chest collapsing, and my own words come in echoes.

"So much, so much."

I turn toward her, curling my legs underneath me on the seat. "I'm sorry."

Her collapse reverses itself. She stiffens. Her hands fumble over each other. "What are you apologizing for?"

It's my turn to fumble, and I wish I hadn't brought it up. "I . . . well . . . I thought it was my fault that you moved away."

"That makes no sense."

I mess with the drawstring on my hoodie. This is mortifying. Far worse than the time I got my period in ballet class. That was merely embarrassing. Now I'm sludgy with shame. Talking about it feels like being strangled, but Dawn is staring at me with something like wildness behind her eyes. She's hanging on the words I can't seem to form with my leaden lips.

"Tell me," she insists.

I cover my face and speak into my hands. "Your dad . . . he caught us . . . what he saw . . ."

I peer at her through my fingers. She gapes at me, hardfaced. Immediately I'm my own half again—separate.

"What are you sorry for?" she snaps, and the anger in her voice is a slap. "For touching me? Am I that disgusting?"

"Oh my god! No! That's not what I meant. I don't think that. Do you?" The fear of being so completely misunderstood sends me into panic mode. I want to shake her until she understands. "I'm sorry because they took you away from me," I blurt.

Dawn's expression morphs again. A storm passing. For a split second, there's something like sunrise. Joy, maybe. Then she changes again to . . . I don't know what . . . Sadness? Pity? Loss?

"I'm sorry," I repeat, putting my face back in my hands.

"I thought you knew."

It is my turn to be confused.

Dawn peels my hands off my face and holds them. Her skin is hot and papery. I wrap my fingers around hers. "He saw more than us," she says. "He caught my mother with your dad."

My stomach clenches into a tight, painful ball. I shake my head in protest.

Dawn shrugs.

"How do you know?" I ask.

"I saw them kissing."

"Before you moved?"

"Yes."

"And after?"

She sighs and lets go of my hands. "We moved to Portland so my parents could get a fresh start, but that didn't last long."

"What do you mean?"

"Your dad came to our house here."

I am not really grasping this. Is it possible that my father drove two and a half hours to have an affair with Dawn's mother? I want to slam my fists into the steering wheel. No—more than that—I want to take this car, Dawn's mother's SUV, and slam it into the retaining wall of this parking lot. Over and over again.

"What else?" I ask, replaying years of stilted conversations, feigned warmth, and barely concealed aggression. Lodged in my brain are my mother's lectures about women needing to be financially secure and her disgust with romantic comedies that end in a wedding.

"What do you mean, what else? My dad ran away to Alaska and found God. My mother cheated on your dad with David. You and I were collateral damage. That's the plotline."

My family is a set of figurines, a tableau of a family perched on the mantel. My dad looking away. My mother martyred. I'm off to one side in a tutu, completely oblivious to every goddamn thing.

DAWN

Fissures, ruptures, cracks. I hear the rifts forming, hisspopsnap. Thin ice over deep water. The porcelain head of an antique doll. Jessie's face in the light of the carousel. Fragmentation.

She swipes at her eyes with her sleeve, turns the key in the ignition. "We'd better go. It's late. I've got class tomorrow."

She's deadflat and a million miles away. The lines of her face are stiffcreased.

The bright lights of the carousel fade away behind us. I want to bash my head against the dashboard.

I repeat myself. "I thought you knew."

"I do now."

She drives to the transit station, hands over the keys. Her lips brush my cheek, but the kiss is a throwaway, absent of intention. "Drive safe," she murmurs.

I want to wait with her until the MAX train comes, but she refuses, sits down alone, puts in earbuds. As I'm driving away, I watch her in the rearview mirror, pulling pins out of her bun and letting her hair fall around her shoulders. A thin slip of girl.

A shard.

She slices right through me.

I think of the bumblebee ring and the carousel and how we had very nearly found our way back to that other place, the one where we fit together. Once again, our parents have wrecked us.

Zanesville.

This is the thought I carry upstairs to my room after my mother yells and David yells and the keys are requisitioned and I'm told that if I take the car again they will call the police.

My mother: "I was worried."

The stepfather: "I could charge you with theft."

Zanesville.

That is the name that spewed from Hobart's uglyfilthmouth.

I Google.

I search.

I find.

First the picture, taken ten years ago—

The background: a regular old barn with a corrugated metal roof and a lush green field. Bucolic, serene. I expect a couple—boy and girl, of course; hand-in-hand, of course—to spread a checkered picnic blanket and feed each other grapes.

The foreground: trampled mud and a pile of carcasses. Lions with bloody muzzles. A black bear limpsprawled. Tigers . . . not just one . . . but many. Their paws are as big as my head. Their fur is red-stained, mud-stained, defiled.

The man: a sixty-two-year-old white guy with jowls and the blotchy red complexion of an alcoholic. He could be any old guy with grabby hands and an imminent sense of his own mortality. He could be Hobart.

And he owned the animals.

So many animals.

One afternoon, in debt and convinced his wife was cheating on him, the man opened the cages, sat in a pile of raw chicken, and shot himself. And the animals, unexpectedly free from wire and chain link, breached the perimeter.

The first responders had no choice.

A tally of the dead:
eighteen Bengal tigers
seventeen lions
six black bears
three mountain lions
two grizzly bears
one wolf
one baboon

It is almost a Christmas carol, one that makes vomit rise. The person I want to tell is Jessie because she's the only one who might get it, who might see me rattling the cage. But Jessie won't want to see me again. Not after I told her things she didn't need or want to know.

My mother knocks and comes in without waiting for my response. Her eyes flicker to the computer screen, the blood, the gore. "What is that?"

"Zanesville."

"Are you doing your schoolwork?"

"No."

She straightens the blankets on my bed, smoothing the wrinkles with long fingers, and sits on the edge of it. "You have to pass that class to keep your slot in the fall."

I don't say anything.

"We can't keep doing this."

I know. I agree. I say nothing.

No one wants this. Least of all me. When I'm here, I knock up against the edges of her world. BodyBeautiful™ will crush the life out of me.

"What are we going to do?" she asks. Her concern is suffocating.

As if I knew. The clock is running out on my time at home. David won't stand for it much longer.

"I overheard you talking to Dad."

She sits very still, her back rigid.

"I wouldn't hurt them."

Her face is a careful mask. "That's what I told him."

"I wouldn't hurt them," I say with more emphasis.

"How do you know?"

Her question is dovesoft, whisperlight. The gentlest of accusations.

My hands in my lap are small, flimsy things—like children—easily bent and broken. Not paws and claws. Who is afraid of a sick girl, a trapped girl?

"My hands hurt." Immediately, I know it's not the right thing to say. In fact, it is the exact wrong thing. I see my mistake in the lift of her shoulders, the way her face falls and cracks and she doesn't even care if she looks ugly or not.

The scales have tipped.

I lose.

She has decided David and the doctors are right. This is all in my head. Probably I'm just fucking with them. Every bruise and every ache is a scam, a cry for attention.

A dead end.

A waste of her mothering.

And this knowledge hurts far more than my hands.

"I am making an appointment with a psychiatrist," she says.

"Okay."

A glance darts my way, quick, suspicious. She doubts my acquiescence.

"Why did you do it?" I ask. "Why did you cheat on Dad?"

She leaves my room without a word.

I read every article I can find about what happened in Zanesville.

So many bodies.

My body.

A carnage.

JESSIE

The next week goes by in a blur.

I fall into bed exhausted each night, wake like a corpse, and drag myself to the studio. This fatigue goes beyond the body. My mind chews everything apart—my father's affair, Vadim's demands, the bumblebee ring on my finger—but the only thing I can control is my body so I push harder than ever before. I wear out pointe shoes like they are made of corn flakes. I have to ask my mother for more money to buy more.

I do not hear from Dawn.

I do not reach out.

DAWN

7:00 a.m. I wake from disintegrated dreams. None of the bits makes sense, but I write them in the journal anyway. I am trying to apply ethology to the science of myself.

7:25 a.m. Hunger. Food.

7:55 a.m. Automated reminder: Online discussion for OB-012 Advanced Topics in Animal Behavior begins in five minutes. Participation required for successful completion of class.

My required participation is a common theme.

I log in as McCormick and wait for the rest of the class to join. I watch their handles pop on the screen, one by one, faceless names for people scattered across the country.

DrK: Heads up, everyone. Let's get started. You're not graded on content so be brave. Throw ideas out there. Keep it clean. Keep it nice. Say hello so I know you're out there.

MandyJ: Hi, everybody!

Xtra: In the house

BigDuane: Hey, hosers!

Lori: Here

Shane: Yup

McCormick: Present

DrK: Great! Let's get started. I know you're all working on the ethograms. My goal with that assignment is to give you an appreciation for how challenging it can be to collect quality data on animals, especially in the wild.

BigDuane: No kidding, man. Squirrels can freaking hoof it when they want to.

DrK: Indeed!

MandyJ: I saw a great blue heron catch and eat a chipmunk.

Lori: Gross.

DrK: Cool, but that's one data point. Imagine the effort required to document dietary habits for the species.

MandyJ: Ten years of wading in swamps?

DrK: Something like that.

Shane: Jane Goodall was in the jungle for like a hundred years.

DrK: Ha! Okay, on to today's topic. Going big picture, folks. In 1973, evolutionary biologist Theodosius Dobzhansky said, "Nothing in biology makes sense except in the light of evolution." Thoughts about what this means?

Lori: Evolution shaped everything we see in the biological world.

DrK: Good start. Other ideas?

Xtra: Creationists are out of luck.

BigDuane: Fistbump, dude. Taking out the Bible thumpers.

Shane: If we want to explain a biological phenomenon, that explanation needs to have an evolutionary foundation.

DrK: Excellent. Shane and Lori have delineated the two sides of this coin. (1) Biodiversity is a product of evolution and (2) when we see a heron eat a chipmunk, we ask, "What are the evolutionary forces at work?"

McCormick: But isn't the scale of those two things totally different?

DrK: Can you expand on that?

McCormick: One heron eats one chipmunk. Sucks for the chipmunk but there are a hundred thousand others. You're saying if we want to understand why herons eat chipmunks and why that chipmunk was the one that got eaten, evolution can help us.

DrK: Yeah, that's what Dobzhansky's saying.

McCormick: But biodiversity is huge—all the different species that have ever existed on earth from fruit bat to earthworm were produced by the same process.

MandyJ: That's what the creationists hate.

DrK: You've nailed one of the key distinctions: microevolution vs. macroevolution. The former is easier to understand . . .

McCormick: . . . and measure . . .

DrK: But Darwin's book is called *On the Origin of Species*

McCormick: My father believes in seven days of creation.

DrK: Many do. Thoughts from the rest of you?

Shane: There is lots of evidence against the seven day scenario. The fossil record for one.

MandyJ: You can believe anything but science is different.

When the discussion group ends, Dr. Kerns sends a follow-up assignment.

From: Dr. Stephen Kerns
To: Class Roster, OB-012 Advanced Topics in Animal Behavior
RE: Microevolution

Define (micro) evolution.

Evolution is the change in gene frequencies over time.

A mutation changes a gene, which changes a trait.

If the new trait is an improvement, the gene spreads through increased survival or reproduction. If the trait is defective, it fails to spread.

There you go.

Evolution in a nutshell.

How would you know if a mutation was good or bad? The evidence required to make such a distinction would be in future generations, long after you were dead. That seems like a blow to self-observation. Nonetheless, I have decided to conduct some experiments. I want to induce the fugue state.

Experimental protocol #1:
sleep deprivation
minimum length, seventy-two hours

I lie under a tree in the forest thinking about mutation.

I have not slept in twenty-eight hours, twenty-seven minutes.

The morning skybits I see through the branches are gray blue. The tree's bark is shaggy red. Giant sequoia, an ancient species, a survivor, *Sequoiadendron giganteum*. I want to say this name over and over and over. The layer of shed needles beneath me is thick and soft and slightly damp and somewhat prickly. I try not to move too much.

Nothing happens.

I don't go dark.

After a few hours I drag myself back to the house where my mother is waiting to take me to the psychiatrist. She drives with both hands, too agitated to tap. If she squeezes any harder, I think the wheel will snap under the pressure.

"What color is it?" I ask.

Her head whips toward me in the passenger seat and back to the road. "What are you talking about?"

"Your nail polish."

She flicks on the radio and attacks the dial. Country station. Rejected. Christian music. Also rejected, along with my dad. She settles on a talk radio show for half a minute before slamming the whole thing off with her palm and going back to the death grip.

"Looks like pink," I say.

She grits her teeth. "It's called Aurora Blush."

"Pink," I repeat and recline the seat.

It takes several minutes for her to manage a sentence. "Why do you do that?"

"Do what?"

"Needle people," she snaps. I think sparks might start flying out of the top of her head.

I offer synonyms. "Goad, provoke, pester, bait, infuriate."

"Goddamnit!" she says, hitting the steering wheel and making the car swerve.

I didn't realize I had spoken aloud. The lack of sleep is punching holes in everything. I wonder if a fugue is coming. My vision is messed up, but not like it has been. It's more like focus trouble, and the lids keep wanting to close. I spend the rest of the drive to the psychiatrist's office pinching my forearms to stay awake. When we get there, the skin is covered with half-moon-shaped indentations.

My mother does all the things—forms, money, pleasantries—and avoids eye contact with anyone in the waiting room. Two others: a middle-aged Asian man in an eye patch and a pregnant woman. None of us wants to be here. When the time comes, my mother has ten minutes alone with the doctor then I'm ushered back to join them.

Dr. Stubens is:
normal's definition of normal
dark hair, a touch of gray
plaid shirt, no tie, pressed navy trousers, scuffed shoes
a little younger than my mom

He shakes my hand and his fingers are cool. Maybe he has circulation problems. He smiles as if my mother told him about a different daughter. Maybe she did. Maybe she wishes she could. Maybe there is another daughter. There's barely enough networking left in my brain for me to swallow down nonsense.

My mother's name is Monica:
she's never had another child
no wonder she wants a do-over

"How's it going today, Dawn?" Dr. Stubens asks.

I tilt my head toward one shoulder. "I'm tired of going to doctors."

He chuckles, not unkindly. "I'm sure you are. This has got to be frustrating for you."

I gesture toward my mother. "She's frustrated. I'm done."

Dr. Stubens nods as if that makes sense to him, indicates we should sit, and then sits himself.

I say, "There is a long list of things I am not, but no one can tell me what I am."

"A diagnosis," my mother corrects. "That's what we need."

"I've looked through the records you sent," he tells my mother. To me, he says, "Lots of doctors. No wonder you're exhausted."

"I haven't slept in almost thirty-three hours."

My mother launches out of her seat. "What?"

He palms her back into place and gives me a probing look. "Why is that?"

"She's self-destructive, that's why. Look at this!" My mother wrenches the sleeve of my shirt up to my elbow. He leans in to get a look at the nail marks. "She stole the car. She's a danger to herself and others. You have to do something about her."

Dr. Stubens calms her. "Hold on. Let's take everything down a notch. I'd like to talk to Dawn alone." My mother splutters as he shows her to the waiting room. My eyelids surrender to gravity, and I'm almost asleep sitting up by the time he returns. His hand on my shoulder startles me awake. "Do you want a cup of tea?"

"No. I'm going to pace."

"Sounds good."

His office is bigger than my bedroom, and the window overlooks the river. "Nice view," I say.

"Can you tell me about your arms?"

We both look at the reddened half circles.

"I was trying to stay awake."

He makes himself tea from an electric kettle on a table beside his desk. "What's that about?"

"Sleep deprivation can induce altered states of consciousness."

"It's also an effective torture technique."

I stop pacing. "Are you making fun of me?"

"No. I'm stating a fact. Keep people up for extended periods of time and their normal boundaries collapse."

My pulse ratchets up a notch. "Exactly! That's what I'm trying to do."

"Torture yourself?"

"I'm trying to induce the fugue state."

He steeples his fingers in front of his chin. "Ah, I see. What do you hope to achieve?"

"Research. Data collection. Repeatability."

"I thought you wanted them to go away."

I go back to pacing. There's a thought knocking against the inside of my skull. I consider trepanation to remove it.

Trepanation: the use of a medical saw called a trephine to remove a disk of bone from the skull.

The good doctor waits on me and doesn't watch the clock. There's a fluid looseness to my limbs like the ligaments are melting. Exhaustion smears across everything. A scattershot of senseimages blasts across my field of view: black fur, musk, sweat both sweet and sour, the curve of Jessie's neck, the wetscratch of fern fronds against my legs, soil, drywall, rot, sky.

Dr. Stubens clears his throat. "Dawn? Are you still with me?"

Words come hard, clotting in the convolutions of my brain.

"Yes. I did. I am. I mean . . . I did want them to go away, but now I'm not so sure."

Steam curls from the mug. His fingers, long fingers,

encircle the cup. When he drinks, the laryngeal prominence slides up then down, a bulge, a bump, the concealed voice. I realize how tired I am of talking.

He eases me into it. "It says in the notes that you don't remember anything after a fugue state, that you wander and don't know where you are."

"I think that's true for a lot of us."

His low laugh is a soothing sound, the kind I could sleep to. "I think you're right."

This makes me want to tell him things.

I stand at the window and watch the river, a seethingsilver where the flat light hits it. Rain is coming. I smell it through the glass. "The fugues are different now."

"How so?"

"At first, it was blank—lights off, a time hole. Now I wake with the taste of honey in my mouth. I'm raw from being wrenched out of a skin that actually fits me." I pick at my body, pinching and pulling at my arms, my legs, my face. "This, this flesh, it is not what I am supposed to wear." Turning toward him is like moving through sludge. "I wake to walls and bars and chains, and I want to go back."

"I think you should try to sleep," he says.

"What are you going to tell my mother?"

"Have you been taking any illegal drugs?" He holds his hands up before I can protest too loudly. "I don't care about weed so much, but what about hallucinogens? LSD, PCP, mushrooms?"

"They're on the list."

Dr. Stuben raises an eyebrow. "You're planning ahead?"

I shrug. "I was going to start with peyote, but I don't know where to get any."

"Me neither." This conversation appears normal for him. "Is this part of your experimentation? If so, you should know that psychoactive drugs can interact with mental illness in unpredictable ways. Big red flag for me. I want to keep you safe."

The thirty-three vertebrae in my back go rigid. "So you've found a hole to shove me in?"

"I'm not following you."

"I've read up. Schizophrenia, dissociative amnesia, identity disorder, depersonalization-derealization disorder. They all can cause fugues." I'm poison-tongued. I want to lick him and watch him writhe. "You and my mother have so many good options."

"Dawn, I'm not offering any of those diagnoses, and I'm certainly not consulting with your mother about them. I'm saying that certain drugs and certain conditions are volatile together."

"Fine." I'm still mad, but my back goes supple again. "I'll postpone the hallucinogens until you're done analyzing my head."

"Excellent. Now about your head . . . sleep needs to happen. I can give you something for that." The pills are tempting. Not that I need them, but an escape hatch may become necessary. Before I can answer, he says, softkind, "It is not a crime to care for yourself."

Instantly I'm thinking about waxed legs and exfoliated feet, flaxblonde highlights and Aurora Blush. I choke on BodyBeautiful™, coughing like my lung is coming up.

Dr. Stubens hands me a bottle of water from the table with the teakettle. "Are you okay?"

The water goes down. Slickwet, a truth serum.

"No. Not okay. Not even close. I'm suffocating."

He wants more, asks more. He is trying to help. I get that, but mouthsounds and meaning are not coming together for me anymore.

"Sometimes it feels like life is moving too fast," he says. "It would be nice if we could slow it down, get enough of a break to find our footing again."

My head is nodding, but I'm already being swept downstream.

What I need is to inhabit the place that tastes like honey, a body that loves what it loves.

JESSIE

When I show up for rehearsal on Friday afternoon, the mirrors and the windows are covered with sheets, and there is a man in one corner sitting cross-legged on the floor. He has a mane of thick white hair. The muscles in his arms are sinewy. He's drawing with wide, open strokes on a sketch pad in his lap.

The techno is blaring.

Vadim is arranging three large white blocks on the floor. As I prep my toes, he shifts the blocks, stands back to observe, and returns to adjust them. Two are quite close together. The other is behind, maybe eight feet away.

"What do you think, Thom?" Vadim asks the artist.

"Good perspective from here." He flips to a fresh page and turns his charcoal on me. His eyes trace my contours, his blind fingers replicating curves and lines. This is far worse than mirrors. I stiffen.

"Act like I'm not here," he says.

Yeah, like that's going to happen.

Thom turns a new page and fixes his gaze on Nita.

I tighten the final knot on the ribbons of my pointe shoes and join Vadim in the center of the room. "What's with the sheets?"

"You look in the mirror too much."

I immediately bristle. "Isn't that the whole idea?"

"No." He adjusts one of the blocks. They are made of some kind of firm foam, not exactly square but squarish with rounded edges and angles that are not quite ninety degrees. They could pass for ottomans in outer space.

"There's an audience when we perform."

"It's not for them," he says, as if this explains everything.

"Then who's it for?" I ask.

Vadim glares at me. "I thought you were smarter than that."

Screw you, I think, and start warming up for another two hours of this dance that is not ballet. The other girls join me. We don't talk. The artist draws. Vadim paces, muttering, and puts us to work. He positions Nita and Mimi on the two blocks that are close together. "Face different ways," he says. "For this, do not think that the mirrors are the front. We are not front, not back. We are all around." He has them sit with their backs touching, legs spread, lounging like a guy might but with their feet en pointe.

Vadim circles, examining them from all angles.

"Take your hair down."

Mimi blanches. Nita reaches uneasily for the hairpins holding her bun together.

"Do it."

When my hair tumbles down to the middle of my back in tangles I feel naked and bed rumpled.

Vadim nods his approval and repositions all of us.

Thom begins another sketch.

"You two can never stop touching," Vadim tells Mimi and Nita. Nita's head whips toward him. "What? How can we dance like that?"

He sits on the other block and calls me to him. He taps his chest. "We dance from here. Now lean against me back to back." To Mimi and Nita, he says, "Watch."

When he rises off the block, his shoulder slides across my hip. He replaces it with his arm. All the while his lower body is twisting so by the time his hand is on my shoulder, the rest of him has spiraled free. "Contact. That is what I want." He pulls me close, contracting so that his body arches over mine. Instead of feeling safe, I feel like prey, and I slip free, sinuously except for one hand, which I press against his abdomen, holding him at arm's length.

"Exactly," Vadim breathes. "You must touch your partner, but you do not want to. Let that infuse your motion." He sheds my hand, drawing a path up my leg with the inside of his own. Our knees lock together. "Lean back," he says.

When I do, the grappling forces of his weight against mine hijack my body. Freed from the mirrors, something strange happens. Suddenly it's no longer about what I look like or the shapes I make in space. It's not about the right steps at the right time.

My brain shuts off.

An animal energy courses through me.

This is like what happened the first time but even more intense.

The dance is all body.

When I see Vadim's arm sweep toward my waist, I evade and strike back, sliding my leg over his shoulder. When he lifts me, I use my weight to create opposite tension, ignoring the chance that he might drop me.

Again and again, I approach, and he repels my advances. Our roles switch, reverse, change again. By the time we stop, both of us are breathing hard. I have the sensation of great size as if I have grown or the world has shrunk. Or maybe the boundaries of my body were illusions.

The studio spins around me. The world is unfocused. Even his face is a blur. Vadim seems to know I'm off-balance, and he keeps one hand on my back until my equilibrium returns.

"Are you okay?" he asks. The rasp of his voice is a wolf's tongue.

I don't know how to answer. I forgot myself, the room, the artist. There is a pile of charcoal drawings in front of him.

"We switch," says Vadim, drawing Nita to him and waving me toward Mimi, "but this time, the touch is what you want. Begin like this." He encircles Nita, pulling her to him like they are about to have sex.

I am instantly jealous, aware of every place their bodies touch. It makes me ravenous. I take Mimi. Palm to palm. Hand to chest. Thigh to thigh. When I touch her, she stiffens and tries to hold a layer of air between us. I lean my full weight against her. I'm taller, threatening almost. She pushes back, breaks away. A rejection that cuts deep.

"What's your problem?" she hisses.

I back away, stung. "I'm sorry." And I am sorry. Everything about this unsettles me. The wildness of it. The way I feel wanton and out of control. "This is hard," I say. "I shouldn't take it out on you."

Mimi's face softens, and I see how these rehearsals are wearing on her too.

I hold out my hand. "Let's just dance, okay?" For a moment, I think she is going to refuse, but she leans in and her loose hair sweeps my shoulders. I recall what I wrote about longing—

I want to be known.
Known for what I am.
Known and loved.

The words are scratched on a piece of paper crumpled at the bottom of my dance bag along with my hunger for Vadim and the way I am drawn to Dawn, who links the past and now.

I fold myself around Mimi's body, desperate to possess her. Her spine is a knobbed arch against my breasts. My fingers skim her delicate rib cage. I'm not Vadim. I'm me, and I want to keep her safe, not possess and overwhelm her. As if she senses this, Mimi stretches, reversing the curl of her spine and extending into an arabesque. Suddenly our only point of contact is her hand on my shoulder and that feels like the whole world. Careful not to disturb her balance, I slide into a deep plié in second position. She deepens the arabesque and presses down on my shoulder.

We are rooted to the ground. I am the trunk. She is the branches.

Breeze-tossed, she swings her leg from arabesque into a strange, crook-shaped attitude en avant. I loop one arm around her thigh and turn her until her leg wraps around my back, and I rise up out of plié like I am about to take flight.

When the music ends, Vadim is satiated. He rubs his hands together. "Let us see what you have done, Thom."

The artist sets his charcoal down and rubs the black smudges from his hands onto his pants. He stands and gives half of the stack of sketches to Vadim. The two of them fan the drawings out on the floor until the studio is covered with sheets of paper.

I am stunned at how much Thom has captured.

Looking at myself rendered in streaks of black and gray is nothing like watching in the mirror. Instead of seeing a myriad of tiny flaws that must be beaten into perfection, I see myself claiming the territory of the body.

With Nita, hunger.

With Vadim, power.

With Mimi, tenderness.

I have never, until this moment, understood what dance could be.

I am far bigger than the skin that holds me.

DAWN

11:37 p.m.

Lights out, dark out, window up. Just in case.

On the floor, cross-legged, no furniture to crash into. Just in case.

Experimental protocol #2:
rapid inhalation and exhalation, 30 seconds
breath hold, as long as possible

I start the stopwatch on my phone and hyperventilate. Twenty seconds in the phone buzzes, interrupting the experiment and inducing normal breathing patterns. It's Jessie. Her name jumps off the screen and pierces me. There's been no contact since the night on the carousel. I'd given up.

"What are you doing?" she asks, before I say anything. "Did I wake you? I'm sorry."

My lungs recover. All that comes out of my mouth is her name. "Jessie, Jessie."

"It's me."

The tidal wave of shock ebbs, leaving a washed-clean beach.

"Dawn, are you still there?"

"I'm surprised," I say. "I didn't think I'd hear from you again."

It's her turn to pause and process. Finally, she says, "You feel like home."

I wallowbask in the starburst warmth of home, home, home.

I must stay quiet too long because Jessie is stammering a new apology. "I don't mean our parents or the houses we live in or Olympia or anything like that. I mean . . ."

"I know what you mean."

The desperation leaves her voice. "You do?" she whispers.

"There's a place in me that fits you."

Her relief is palpable. "So what are you doing up this late?"

"Oxygen deprivation."

She laughs, and I want to eat the sound of it.

"Seriously," I say. "Hypoxia can induce altered states of consciousness."

"So can LSD."

"That's on my list of things to try." I get up off the floor and lie down on the bed. I have no intention of passing out now.

"Explain!"

I like how she tells me what to do.

"I am trying to make myself black out."

"I'm afraid to ask about the rest of your list."

"Sleep deprivation, hallucinogens, hypnosis, sensory deprivation, nitrogen narcosis, extended eye-gazing."

"What's eye-gazing?"

"I need a partner for that one. Two people sit facing each other and stare at each other's faces for ten minutes."

"And?"

"Supposedly it induces hallucinations, weird thoughts, higher consciousness."

"Can we get together again?" she asks. "I know it's hard because of the car and everything but I want to see you and . . ."

"Sunday?" I blurt. "I have to go to the zoo."

"You are like the queen of non sequiturs, you know."

She's funny and I laugh and rub the bridge of my nose and think maybe doing Dr. Kerns's assignment at the zoo will be the best thing to ever happen to me.

"I prefer to think I make larger neural leaps than lesser humans," I say.

There's a lightness to her voice when we say good night, a comfortplace that holds her long-dead golden retriever and our tree fort in the cherry tree. It's a homeplace, a nowplace.

I tuck the journal in the drawer under my vibrator.

No more experiments tonight.

I'm going to sleep with my phone.

Just in case.

JESSIE

On Sunday morning, I take the MAX train to the west side of town where the zoo is. There's a crowd of protestors gathered when I arrive. They pace back and forth, carrying signs. A man not much older than me with a dirty blond ponytail shoves a photograph of an elephant in my face. "Did you know that Tuva has a perpetually infected tusk?"

I scan the crowd looking for Dawn. He jams another photograph into my hand. The image is of wrinkled, gray, lacerated skin. It's an elephant foot pocked with pus-filled sores.

"Look at their feet!" he shouts. "Look what captivity does to them."

The ripped flesh on my own feet throbs.

Dawn's mom pulls up in her SUV, rolls down the window, and waves. "Hi, Jessie!"

I respond with a pasted-on stage smile, unsure of the protocol when greeting your father's hookup. Dawn gets out of the car, holding a clipboard and scowling.

"I'll be back in two hours," her mom says and pulls away from the curb.

As soon as she's gone, Dawn takes a big breath and cracks her neck and says, "Good riddance."

"Is it that bad?"

"Yes."

She puts the clipboard between her knees and takes off her flannel shirt. Underneath she's wearing a black T-shirt that stretches across her shoulders. Her body is different. It's been less than two weeks since I saw her, but she's more muscular and sinewy. The change is striking. "Have you been working out?" I ask.

She gives me a weird look. "Why would I do that?"

"To get ripped, I guess."

"Low on my priority list."

"Okay, but—"

Before I can ask her what's going on, she takes the picture out of my hand and says, "Asian elephant. *Elephas maximus.* Hind foot. Right side. Those are terrible lesions."

I gape at her.

"P. T. Barnum said, 'When entertaining the public, it is best to have an elephant.'" Her quoting voice has knives in it. "When they're caged, their feet go to mush."

"Horrible."

"I know."

We thread our way through the crush of people. It's chaos. Young mothers push strollers. Toddlers bolt out of their reach. The soundtrack is a hundred different versions of *Mom, Mama, Mommy.* I pass a lost baby sock printed to look like a ballet slipper. The indoctrination starts early.

"I don't like the zoo," Dawn says, walking so close that we almost touch.

"Then what are we doing here?" I ask.

"Homework."

We stop at the elephants. Several stand close together.

Their trunks are in constant motion, caressing one another. I imagine they are mothers and daughters or maybe sisters.

I lean into Dawn. "I missed you."

"After the carousel, after I didn't hear from you, I thought that was it."

"It was a lot to process."

"And then?"

The rail around the elephant enclosure is cold metal under my arms. Inside, the animals stand on concrete. I am worried about their feet.

"The dance I am doing in the showcase is very unusual. It's hardly ballet at all. It dredges things up for me."

"Like what?"

I shake my head. "I don't know how to explain, but it reminds me of what we had, what it meant to have someone like you." The elephants lean into each other as if they need the support to remain standing.

Dawn slides an arm around me and whispers, "It was good."

The primate house has been partially remodeled. Outside, each species has a large netted enclosure open to the sky with trees and plants and real dirt. A simulation of nature with an observation platform for zoo visitors. Inside is still institutional concrete and metal. The paint is chipped off the cinder-block walls, and there are metal bars and a layer of glass between us and them. It's humid inside the viewing hall. The heavy air is laced with the smell of fruit on the verge of going bad. Gibbons hang from knotted ropes. An orangutan dismembers a cardboard box. A male baboon slides his bulbous bottom along the glass. Two boys snicker and point.

Dawn leads me to the chimpanzee enclosure and holds

out a clipboard. On the printed form, she has labelled the columns with a series of behaviors like *eating, sleeping, grooming self, grooming other.* There are sixty numbered rows on her data collection sheet. One for each minute of an hour-long observation period.

"You're the timekeeper," she says. "I need one-minute intervals. Our job is to check off which behaviors we see in each minute. Let's decide who we're going to watch."

Right now, there are only two chimps in the inside section of the enclosure. One is sleeping on a mesh platform about ten feet off the ground. The other is on the ground, sorting through a pile of leafy branches with long, careful fingers.

"That one," I say.

Dawn studies the interpretive sign that has a photograph and short biography of each inhabitant in the chimp enclosure. "I think that must be Shassa," Dawn says, pointing to a picture of a chimp the exact same color of deep gray as the one on the ground. I read the text: zoo-born and zoo-reared. She has been here for forty years. That might as well be forever. What new thing could the chimp hope to find among the leaves and twigs?

Dawn fills out the top of the form.

Focal animal: *Shassa, female chimpanzee*

Weather: *Sunny outside. Around 65 degrees. Dim inside. Hot. Smells like damp towels.*

I set my phone to count off a series of minutes.

Shassa has reached the bottom of the pile of branches. Lethargically, she scrapes her fingers against the bare concrete. Dawn checks the column marked "other" and writes in the notes section: *I don't know what she's looking for.* The chimp begins to pull off leaves and eat them. Dawn checks "eating."

"New minute," I say, and Dawn moves the tip of her pen to the next row.

A little girl bounces up to the glass, holding a dingy blanket in one hand. She knocks on the glass. Shassa looks up and meets her eyes and the girl squeals. "Look, Mommy. A monkey!"

"That's nice," says her mom, not looking up from her phone.

"Not a monkey. An ape," Dawn mutters.

Shassa eats a mouthful of leaves and then climbs up to the sleeping chimp. Dawn checks boxes. The girl and her mother are gone. Another minute passes. Up on the platform, Shassa nudges the other chimp until it wakes up. This one has freckles. I check the interpretive sign. A young female named Gombe. They groom each other.

While Dawn records our observations, people walk past in fits and starts. Small jumbles of children. Families. A school group. A teenage couple with their arms around each other. None stays longer than a few seconds. The chimpanzee named Shassa has been here for forty years and does not merit more than a sideways glance.

Dawn keeps collecting data.

Shassa climbs back down and settles in to groom herself.

The longer I watch the chimpanzee, the more things I notice. A notch out of one ear. The way she cups her arms around herself. A particular downward curve to her shoulders that makes her seem exhausted.

When I look up from the phone after the next time interval, the chimpanzee is no longer grooming. She is staring at us. The pressure of her gaze is almost unbearable. It's a physical weight, an accusation leveled at our entire species. She finally looks away and relief floods me.

"Did you see that?" I whisper.

Dawn nods. "She knows we're watching her."

It's very clear that our observation is unwelcome. The rest of the hour crawls by. Dawn checks boxes. I murmur the time. At the fifty-second minute, the chimpanzee stands and glares at us. I want to apologize. She didn't ask for this. She didn't want to be on display any more than I wanted to dance Vadim's choreography.

But here we are.

Before the observation time is up, the chimpanzee named Shassa trudges to the farthest corner of the enclosure and sits with her back to us, facing the corner. We all know she's never getting out.

DAWN

We leave her there with her nose against the cinder-block wall of the enclosure. She is a female specimen of the species *Pan troglodytes*, forty years old. The oldest known chimpanzee in captivity is seventy-two. That little girl called her *monkey, monkey, monkey,* and her mother didn't correct her error. She didn't say *chimpanzees are apes.* She didn't say *chimpanzees share ninety-seven percent of our DNA.* She didn't say *we are family.*

Family Hominidae—orangutans, gorillas, bonobos, chimpanzees, and us—tool-makers, language-users, problem-solvers.

Look what we do to family.

Jessie takes my hand, and we leave.

The faces in the crowd blur into a stream of color. Tears? A coming fugue? I am too drained to discern the difference. When my mother comes, Jessie's fingers fall away from mine. My sternum cracks open. I am vivisected and exposed. How convenient for my mother. She can take me to the doctors now, and since my chest cavity gapes wide, they can analyze my entrails for rot or parasites or prophecy.

The elephant protesters are still there.

I think of Zanesville.

And I remember the bear.

JESSIE

After I leave the zoo, I ride the MAX train downtown, but instead of transferring lines to the one that would take me back to Patrice and Ed's house, I walk along the river for a long time, trying to figure out what I am going to do after the spring showcase. Going home will kill me.

DAWN

Before my stepfather returns, I leave the house.

This time of day—dusk, evening, dinner—is the only time it feels like people actually live in this subdivision. Around me is a slide show of other people's lives. Garage doors open. Living room TVs glow. I lope past kitchen windows and dinner preparation. Kidschasedogschaseballs. The scarf of a girl on a bike is a sail, a flag, a celebration.

I am not any of these things.

I am something else.

JESSIE

It's the next day when I hear from Dawn. A text, that's all, but when I see it's from her, a flash of something like hope shoots through me. I open the text, eager.

Dawn has sent a picture of a pillow in the middle of a crumpled bed. There's a big smudge of mud across the white fabric.

It's instantly ominous. The opposite of sexting.

Is that your room? I ask.

Yes.

I ignore the prickling sensation in the back of my neck. I try for levity. You need to clean.

Cleaning is the worst.

Dawn sends another picture. This time a close-up of the muddy fabric. There's hair stuck to it. Coarse, short, wiry black hair.

Ew . . . Are those pubes?

I think an animal got in here.

Dog?

There is a long pause, then she says, Who's been eating my porridge? Who's been sleeping in my bed?

I hold the phone to my chest.

We are on the edge of a precipice, and the height is making me nauseous. I don't know what comes next for either of us, but I'm pretty sure it's not a fairy tale.

You know what? I text. Goldilocks was kind of a twat.

DAWN

8:00 a.m.

Thursday morning

Fugues: three, unrelated to experimental induction

Number of days since I've seen Jessie: four

Our texts: eighty-seven, words that knit us back together

From: Dr. Stephen Kerns

To: Class Roster, OB-012 Advanced Topics in Animal Behavior

RE: This week's writing assignment

Describe an example of microevolution in the real world.

From: Dawn McCormick

To: Dr. Stephen Kerns

RE: Microevolution

Another creation story:

She's doomed.

That's the short story.

Let me paint the picture for you. She's forty-two years old, a runner, a mother, a teacher, *Homo sapiens*. She's clutching the white rim of the toilet, puking her guts up. It's been coming out the other end too. She's five-foot-eight inches tall and weighs one-hundred-forty pounds. She's been hijacked by the bacterial colony in her digestive tract—a virulent strain of *Escherichia coli*.

No biggie, you say. Throw some antibiotics at her. Fix her right up.

The drugs get to work. A sniper's run, killing bacteria left and right.

Except not all of the bacteria have exactly the same genetic code. Mutation has done its random dirty work, flipped some base pairs. An adenine becomes a guanine. The meaning changes.

Most of the bacteria with mutated code are defective, can't do shit, single-celled losers in the game of life. But there's one, lucky bastard. This bacterium has a mutation that makes it resistant to the antibiotic flooding the teacher's system.

The rest die, but this one replicates, reproduces, multiplies, fills the teacher and she is sicksicksick, probably dies. And presto change-o, microevolution creates a superbug.

And when my father quotes Genesis—*Let us make man in our image, after our likeness. And let him have dominion over the fish of the sea and over the birds of the heavens and over the livestock and over all the earth and over every creeping thing that creeps on the earth*—I think he is confused about who has dominion over whom.

From: Dr. Stephen Kerns

To: Dawn McCormick, Student ID # 91967

RE: Microevolution assignment

Dear Ms. McCormick,

Obviously you have an excellent grasp on the material we are covering. Kudos for that. I want to remind you that a more formal writing style is expected in rigorous academic settings, especially Stanford. Please adhere to that format in all future work. Also, references are required. Follow *Chicago Manual of Style* conventions.

Best,

Dr. Kerns

I format my sources and send them to Dr. Kerns, and I don't include a single expletive.

JESSIE

With the performance only a few weeks away, our rehearsal schedule has doubled. The foyer is a hurricane of Band-Aid wrappers, hair bands, and snippets of pink satin ribbon. There is little time for anything else. We dance, eat, sleep, repeat.

Eduardo is finishing up when I arrive. I watch the end of his rehearsal with an odd detachment. The piece is lovely. Especially Lily's part. Every single movement she makes is exquisite. The dance blooms around her, unfolding with neither conflict nor tension.

The piece does not make my stomach churn. It does not provoke or arouse me.

I appreciate it, admire it even, but I am shocked to realize that I no longer want it.

It is very, very safe.

When they finish and the other girls spill into the foyer, Lily sits on the couch next to me.

"How's rehearsal been going?" I ask.

"It's going well. I like my part."

"You'd better," Brianna spits. "It's the best one."

Lily wilts around the edges.

"Ignore that bitch," I say.

She un-wilts a little. Lily pats my arm, tucks her pointe shoes in her dance bag, and heads for the door. "See you tomorrow."

Brianna gives me the middle finger. "How's your freak dance, freak?"

"Too much for you to handle," I say, giving her the finger back.

Vadim calls us into the studio to get started. We warm up quickly, forgoing the barre and moving right into the center. When we're slick with sweat, Vadim shifts into the choreography.

He is calling the piece *Turbulence.*

I plunge into the movements, acting and reacting. In the dance, equilibrium is a shifting target. Amid the force of our collisions and the gravitational pull of our desires, it takes everything to dance this way.

Tonight, it's dark by the time Vadim releases us.

Mimi and Nita head home. Vadim disappears into the men's dressing room. I'm alone in the studio, exhausted but still immersed in the territory of the dance. After each rehearsal it is hard for me to extricate myself. It's like I have to rediscover who I am every single time.

And when I do, my worries about the future come barreling back.

I'm starting to wish I could stay lost.

I sit on the floor of the studio, kneading the constricted muscles in my calves. I can't seem to muster the energy for the walk to the train station. It's cold and wet and late, and I have to be back here by nine tomorrow morning. I contemplate sleeping on the couch in the foyer.

"What are you still doing here?" Vadim asks. He has changed into tight jeans and a gray sweater that looks like cashmere. There's a leather jacket hooked over one of his fingers. He slouches against the doorjamb, drinking me in.

"I was wishing I didn't have to go home," I say.

"Is that so?"

Suddenly the air in the studio is charged.

He crosses the wood floor to where I sit and holds out his hand. When I take it, he lifts me to my feet and pulls me into him. We have touched a hundred times in rehearsal.

But not like this.

His jacket falls to the floor.

I run my hands across the cashmere. His chest is taut underneath, and I weave my arms around his neck.

"Jessie," he says, hungry and hard.

His face is end-of-day rough against my cheek. His hands slide down my back, my ass. He presses himself against me. The kiss is hard and deep, and I feel it all the way down to the soles of my feet.

I fold myself into him. The soft bits—his lips, behind his ears, the insides of his wrists—and the hard bits too. I want all of them.

We kiss until I'm blind with the lust of it.

After I don't know how long, Vadim peels us apart.

"Put this in the dance," he says. "This is what I need from you."

My own need is a hurricane. The absence of his mouth on mine physically hurts. Every inch of me vibrates.

"I want—"

He touches my lips with his finger. "I know. So do I. But the dance is what matters." He slides his finger between my breasts and all the way down to the top of my mound. "And you are its very core."

I reach for him, ravenous.

But Vadim retreats and says softly, "Get your things, love."

He picks up his jacket and hands me my pointe shoes.

I tug on sweatpants and collect the rest of my stuff. One by one, Vadim turns off the lights, plunging the studio into darkness. He ushers me out the door and sets the alarm.

"Are you taking the MAX?" he asks.

I nod, and he walks me to the station. When the train comes, I ride home hungry. I want more than the dance. I want to slide myself along Vadim's bare chest. I want to be huge and invincible. I want to eat the world. I want to burst into flames.

What I've got is a stained seat on the train and another rehearsal first thing tomorrow.

At home, I get in the shower and let the heat pepper my shoulders. Steam fills the tight space. I close my eyes and let one finger circle my breast. My nipples are hard and tingling. When my finger slips down into the slit of my crotch, it's slick and hot, and I rub myself until I come.

The bathroom cools around me. I put on my robe and make my way back to the bedroom. Soon the showcase will be over, and I will have to figure out what I am going to do.

I text Dawn.

She doesn't answer.

I send another message and another.

I don't want you to be sick, I say.

What I mean is don't leave me alone again.

DAWN

Saturday, 10:35 a.m.

My mother is holding a BodyBeautiful™ brunch downstairs. Mimosas bubble. Adornment proceeds. I pace. It has been nearly two weeks since Jessie and I went to the zoo. She is busy with preparations for the spring showcase. I've kept my promise to Dr. Stubens. No hallucinogens. Not yet.

I slept seven hours and twelve minutes last night.

In these four walls.

I haven't had a fugue in five days.

I haven't left the house. At least not that I know of.

The subdermal alterations to my body are becoming more pronounced. Even David will notice the changes. I have to get out of here.

I reread an article about eye-gazing from the *Journal of Psychiatric Research*.

Twenty test subjects, all strangers to each other, were paired at random and told that they were going to undertake a meditative experience. The instructions were easy: stare into each other's eyes for ten minutes. You can blink, but don't look away. You can sit close, but don't touch. During the experiment, most participants noted changes in visual acuity, amplified hearing, an altered perception of the passage of time, and visual hallucinations.

This all sounds very familiar.

Some also noted elevated feelings of connection with their partners. Some called it love.

If only.

The explanation for what is happening to me lies in the fugue. I'm sure of it. Maybe eye-gazing is the way to get myself there.

But I am alone, like always.

In my room.

Four walls.

How can I do the experiment?

I text Jessie. Can you help me with another project? And realize after I send it that she is in ballet class and won't see it until at least noon. Besides, the all-consuming showcase of doom is coming.

Downstairs, there's a peal of laughter. Are they debating the merits of shaving versus waxing? Mascara versus extensions? I imagine barging in and begging one of the ladies to gaze into my eyes for six hundred seconds. I can guess how that would go down.

They'd rather stare at their own reflections.

I pace some more.

Then the answer hits me.

Of course.

A mirror.

I don't keep one in my room and that means opening the door and letting in the sound of my mother and her friends and walking through a cloud of perfume. In her bathroom, my mother keeps a freestanding makeup mirror. It lights up around the edges. I set it up on the desk in my room.

Experimental protocol #3:
dim lighting
mirror-gazing, ten minutes
alone

I turn off the overhead light, lock the door, and shut the shades. My room is a dark cave, lit only by the glowing edges of the mirror. I settle into the desk chair and start the stopwatch on my phone.

My face seems to float in the dark background.
First thought: I don't want to look at my own face.
Second thought: it's not the right face.
Third thought: ten minutes is a long time.

At first it is hard not to look away. The longer I stare the more my reflection wobbles and distorts. The eyeballs rebel, make tears, salt water. It's hard not to blink them away. My lashes stick together.

The face in the mirror looks less and less like me every second. Its features flicker and morph like watching someone through the flames of a fire. Red, orange, me. Not me. Yellow blaze. My mother. Jessie. Me. Not me. The spectrum shifts. Blueflicker, greenblaze, whiteheat.

The face ripples in and out of focus. The forehead broadens, nose lengthens. Teeth sharpen. The glass seems to roll like ocean beyond the wavebreak. I'm there, not there. Here, not here. The bones of my face ache, a dull thud from the inside out.

When I tear my gaze away from the mirror, it is like evisceration, a claw slash from collarbone to pelvis. A spill of hot guts. There's musk in my nose, oily and midnightdark. Pain radiates from under my shoulder blades, down my arms, through my spine. Nothing fits. Not these clothes, that face, this room. I rip out of my jeans, shred my T-shirt pulling it over my head, tear my underwear from my hips.

Naked, I rake at the blinds, and they splinter.

Windowglass, flatclear, hardclosed.

One swipe and it shatters. I'm climbing out. Thighflesh, whitesoft, scored by shards in the frame. Across the wooden patio covering. I land on the deck with a thump. Faces in the living room turn toward me. Circular mouths. The shock of it.

> me here nakedbleeding
> the ladies
> my mother
> they fade
> bone deep upheaval
> smells rise, magnify, explode
> dirtscent leafscent sweetsourbitter

I lumber to my feet, crush through fence and field, push into the forest, a shifting whistling teeming place. Lope toward, change into—

> scraperumblesnuffle
> digscratchdelve
> something new

JESSIE

I've been home long enough to eat and strip out of my clothes and shower. Exhaustion simmers in my limbs. It's almost midnight when my phone rings. A unknown number. I almost don't answer.

But I do and it's Dawn.

"Please—" she says. "Need you."

My whole body stiffens, every fiber on high alert. "What happened?"

"Don't know." Her breath on the other end of the line is hoarse and ragged.

"Where are you?"

She doesn't answer. There's background noise, and suddenly there is someone else on the line, a loud, impatient woman. "Your friend is messed up."

"Who is this?" I ask. "Where's Dawn?"

"We're at a strip club by the airport," says the woman who has no time for me. "You got to get her off my hands. She's freaking out the other girls."

I stand naked in the middle of the room, trying to process this. "Is she okay?"

"I don't think so. Her hands and legs are all cut up."

I grab a pen and a piece of paper. "Tell me the address."

I park Patrice and Ed's Prius between a Cadillac and an F-350. The place is packed. The strip club has red siding and porthole windows, like a squarish jumbo jet, permanently grounded. It's called the Landing Strip, of all things. Phallic columns flank the main entrance. There's a red carpet spread out and ready to slurp me up.

I pull my peacoat tighter around my body and flip the collar up so I can hide in it. Even so, the men hoot at me. One whistles. Another grabs his crotch. "Looking good, baby," he says even though I'm swathed in wool and wearing jeans. Their eyes cling to me as I enter.

It's dark inside, red booths, velvety walls the color of menstrual blood. It's like being inside a giant vagina.

"You got ID?" asks a weasly-faced guy manning the front door.

"I just came to pick up a friend. She's here somewhere." I scan the room. It's mostly men at the bar in front of the stage. Shift workers from the port nearby and off-duty airport employees, I guess. No Dawn. "Maybe she's in the back or something. I'm supposed to ask for Asia."

The bouncer rubs his stubbled cheek. "Well, shit. Why didn't you say so? Wait here." He walks to the back of the club with a weird, fidgety gait that makes me think he's on drugs.

The performer on the stage is all legs and tits and ass and tattoos. Multicolored lights flicker over her as she sways and twists her body, eel-like, around the pole. There's a rhinestone in her belly button. When she bends over, a strip of gold fabric snugs into her crotch.

The bouncer returns and gestures for me to follow him through the door next to the stage. When I pass, the dancer is pressing her breasts together and leaning over the men at the bar. She's wearing platform heels. I wonder if her feet hurt and if she minds the way they look at her.

Backstage it is even darker and dingier. A woman in a thong bikini patterned with the stars and stripes opens the door to the dressing room. "What's up, Jake?" she asks.

He nods his head back toward me. "This girl says she's looking for Asia."

A naked woman who must be six feet tall with huge fake tits comes over.

"Asia," says Jake, his head at boob level, "you've got to get her out of here. She's underage."

The stripper laughs and pats him on the head. Her breasts wobble back and forth. She's a landscape of hills and valleys. She swallows space. "You worry too much, Jake-y Boy. I'll get the little thing out of here as soon as I can."

I notice that she has no pubic hair. Her crotch looks like a little girl, but the rest of her is a lioness. Asia pulls me inside and shuts the door in Jake's face. "You here for your messed-up friend? For Dawn?" She's leaning into me, threatening even while naked.

And mad. She seems mad at me, and I can't imagine why.

"Is she here?" I ask.

Asia purses her lips together and says, "Girl, she could have been killed."

I hold up empty hands. "I have no idea what you're talking about."

"Come here." Asia grabs me by the coat and pulls me past the mirrors where two other dancers are getting ready. One plucks her eyebrows. Another does her makeup. In the far corner of the dressing room is a ratty couch. Someone is curled up on one end under an old patchwork blanket.

"Hey," Asia says, peeling back the blanket.

Dawn is naked. Her skin is nearly translucent. Dark circles cup her eyes. Her cheeks are bruised. A dank, earthy smell rises from her. She's looking right at me, but I don't think she sees me. She reaches out blindly and says my name. "JessieJessieJessie."

I recognize nothing in her eyes, but I take her hand and say, "It's me."

Asia is standing, hands on hips, watching us. "If she is sick, like contagious sick, there is going to be hell to pay. It's not like this shit hole offers benefits."

I don't take my eyes off Dawn. "It's not like that."

"Well, good, because I had her in my car."

"What happened?" I ask Dawn. No answer. She shakes her head weakly, but I don't know if that means she doesn't know or she can't tell me. I keep a hold of her hand and turn back to Asia, who is zipping herself into a purple corset. "Where did you find her?"

We are both in the mirror—me and her, hardly the same species.

"I found that crazy bitch wandering naked along the side of the road. The things that could have happened to her . . ." She says this with such hardness that I guess she knows all too well what can happen to girls in the night.

Dawn moans in the nest of blankets. When I brush the sweat-soaked hair from her forehead, she's burning with fever.

"She on drugs?" Asia asks.

I shake my head. "I don't know."

Dawn pushes feebly at the blanket with bloody hands.

Asia frowns. "Look at her legs."

I don't want to look, but I do. There are cuts all over her

inner thighs. I think I'm going to be sick. "We've got to call the police."

"Absolutely not!" Asia is adamant. "She can't stay here. Neither can you. None of us need any more trouble."

"Okay, we're going," I say, having absolutely no idea what I am supposed to do.

Jake pokes his head through the dressing room door. "Asia. You're on."

She raises a hand in his direction. To me, she says, "You girls gonna be okay?"

"Sure," I say, trying to convince myself. "We've got this."

"Here," says Asia, handing me a T-shirt and a pair of sweatpants. "Your friend can keep them."

I take the clothes. "Thank you for helping her."

She nods. "We've got to stick together, right?"

The last thing she does before heading to the stage is smear Vaseline across her front teeth. It makes my breath catch in my chest. I have done the exact same thing before every performance I have ever danced. It lubricates our lips so we can smile through our exertions. Turns out, Asia and I are not so different after all.

With an arm around her waist, I dress Dawn and help her past the men smoking and into the car. She collapses in the passenger seat, sliding in and out of consciousness. I decide that I have to take her to the hospital, but when I pull into the emergency department at Emanuel, she sits bolt upright and roars at me.

I slam on the brakes.

She clutches my arm, eyes rolling wildly in her head. "They will . . . take . . . me."

"But the cuts . . . you're hurt. You're sick. I need you to be okay."

I'm crying now and can't stop.

Her chest heaves, and her head is twisting this way and that, like an animal in a trap.

"Wait," she begs. She squeezes my arm hard enough to hurt. "Just need . . . rest. I am . . . changing. Not . . . dying. Please."

I don't know what to do. I'm sobbing so hard it feels like bones are breaking. I'm all tears and snot and fear and I don't know what to do. Suddenly, she's crouching on the passenger seat like she's going to pounce. She cups my face in her hands, hard. Bores into me with sharp eyes.

"Stop!"

It's a slap, and I am immobilized by it.

"You have to trust me," she says, completely lucid.

I gulp hard and get control of myself.

"If you take me to the hospital, I won't get out, and that will kill me."

I nod. She lets go of me and slides back into her seat.

"I'll take you to my place," I say, wiping my face on my sleeve. And even though I'm not sure it's the right thing, Dawn is the only person in my entire life that I have ever trusted, and I decide to trust her now.

When we get to the house, I have to shake her awake. She peers at me, heavy-lidded, but gets out of the car and tries to walk. She almost falls, and I catch her around the waist. She leans against me. The weight of her is immense, and again I'm struck by the way her body feels too solid and dense for someone her size.

I help her into the bed, turn out the light, and climb in next to her. I cup her body with my own. Her curved back presses against my chest. Her body begins to thrash. She's paper on fire. Her edges curl and contort.

I stroke her cheek.

I murmur and shush.

Maybe she's having a seizure. I second-guess my decision not to take her to the emergency room.

Dawn claws at Asia's shirt. "Hot," she moans, barely audible. "So hot."

I throw the blankets off the bed. Muscles ripple under her skin even though she's not moving. When I try to move away from her, Dawn's eyes rocket open, the whites visible all around the blue. She reaches for me, chokes out words. "Need . . . you . . ." I wrap myself around her again, and Dawn twitches in my arms.

I remember when our parents separated us.

I remember how we tried to stay together.

"Changing." She gulps, almost chokes, and even though I don't know what she means, I am afraid. She struggles to swallow. Another wave of tremors hits her limbs. Her breath hiccups in her chest. Her nails scrape my arms. The violence in her body builds. A musky, panicked scent rises from her. Her muscles harden. Her face grows wild.

"Stay with me," I beg.

Words judder out through her gritted teeth. "I. Am. Trying."

I hold her more tightly, murmur into her ear, and after what seems like forever, her breathing slows and evens out. The growling rasp is gone. She's no longer feverish. And eventually, we sleep.

I wake, thanking every single god I know that it is Sunday and I do not have to dance. My body is wrecked, sore from rehearsals and cramped from a night bent around Dawn. My clothes are twisted and every seam chafes. If I had to dance today, it might break me.

My friend is still asleep. In the night, we untangled ourselves, and she is curled up like a fetus ready to emerge. One hand lies on top of the blanket. Her nails are chewed to the quick. Her veins stand out, plum-colored.

I ease out of the bed and get in the shower and stand under the hot water for a long time.

What are we supposed to do?

I have no idea.

When I come back in my robe, Dawn is awake. Her face is soft. I've never seen her unguarded like this, not since we were children.

"Hi," I say, suddenly shy, feeling like a kid myself.

"You came. No one else would have."

Who would have come for me? Nita? Vadim? I doubt it. Maybe Patrice. And my dad, I guess. My throat tightens and my eyes sting. I look away, unwrapping the towel from my hair. "Strippers, huh? Didn't know that was your scene."

The whisper of a laugh escapes her.

"What happened?" I say.

Dawn shakes her head and looks momentarily lost.

I am afraid to ask about the blood on her legs, but I have to. "Did someone hurt you?"

She gives me a questioning look.

I point to her body under the blankets. "Look at your legs."

When she pulls down her sweatpants, dried flakes of blood dot the white sheets. She stares at her inner thighs and pokes at the wounds. As I watch she slides one finger inside herself and probes. It pains me to watch her exposed and touching herself, calculating the possibility of trespass.

She meets my eyes. "Doesn't hurt."

I nod and swallow hard. "Good."

She pulls a sliver of glass from one of the wounds and drops it into the palm of my hand. The red-tinged wedge of glass is warm from the inside of her body. I tuck it into a pocket in my dance bag.

"You're beautiful," she says.

I feel myself flush. "That's random."

A soft smile spreads across her face, and she eases into the pile of pillows. The shadow of a bruise lingers on her right temple, a greenish-yellow smudge.

"Are you sure you're okay?" I ask.

She shrugs, a tightness around her eyes.

"Do you want to shower?"

She nods.

When I return from the linen closet in the hall with a fresh towel, her eyes are closed. I can't tell if she's breathing. I kneel by the bed, terrified that she's not. I lean my cheek to her lips. Breath wafts against my cheek. She smells like wet soil and growing things.

Her hand rises, cups the back of my head, pulls me close.

After a moment, she says, "I . . . was trying . . . to find . . ."

Dawn trails off. She's breathing hard like this was too much effort for her battered body.

I sit up so I can look into her eyes. "What? What were you trying to find?"

"Myself."

"And did you?"

Her face changes, a weather pattern promising storms, but she doesn't answer. She doesn't tell me what she found.

I help Dawn into the bathroom, and instead of a shower, I run her a bath. When the tub is full, Dawn's movements are too uncoordinated for her to undress, and I have to help her.

When she's naked, I help her ease into the water.

Dried blood dissolves into pink and swirls away.

She slides down until the surface of the water laps against her breasts. They're dappled with freckles, and her nipples are apricot-colored and hard. I imagine last night, Dawn walking naked along the road, oblivious to who might come. Unconcerned about what might be done to her.

I want to gather her up and keep her close.

"Are you okay in here alone?" I ask.

She nods without opening her eyes.

I leave the bathroom door ajar and get dressed. I strip the sweat-soaked sheets off my bed and start a load of laundry. There's a note from Patrice and Ed on the island in the kitchen downstairs. *Gone waterfall watching in the gorge. Croissants in the bag by the stove. Left you the Prius in case you need it. XO*

I wish the things I worry about were as simple as waterfalls and croissants.

When I come back to my room, Dawn is there, wrapped in a towel. She watches me rummage through the dresser for something she can wear. For a moment we stand close together. Me holding a shirt and a pair of leggings for her. Dawn giving me a look that suggests other things. I think she might kiss me.

I think I want her to.

I like the way she looks at me.

Not as prey. Not as competition or a means to an end.

She sees me.

And I want her to know I see her too, but I've taken too long to show my desire.

Dawn takes the clothes and gently pushes me out of my own room.

By the time Dawn comes downstairs, I've warmed up the pastries and made coffee. We play house over tiny glasses of orange juice and soft cooked eggs. I'm suddenly shy. She doesn't want to talk, but I don't want distance to grow between us again.

"Do you remember our forts?"

All I want is to be nine again in a world made of chairs and blankets, full of stuffed animals and pillows. She touches my hand. So much goes unspoken, but I'm weepy with wanting a place like that fort, a place where I fit.

I pick at a flaky corner of the croissant. "After you left, it was terrible. Without you, there was too much time. I went on pointe at twelve. Danced constantly. It became the only thing I wanted."

"Girls want . . . things," she says with gravel in her voice.

"You used to want to be a vet."

Shadows crash through her face.

"You're really smart," I say. "Stanford and everything. You could be a vet."

Dawn chews slowly, almost like she has to remind herself how to do it. "Maybe."

I refill our coffee mugs. I watch the cream swirl into the dark liquid. This is so adult-y, what we are doing, like suddenly we're all grown up, and we've known each other forever and there was never a time when we were apart. This moment is weirdly golden, a comfort.

Too brief.

"Take me . . . home?" she says.

Tears jab against my eyelids. Again. The fort is dismantled. Not even Dawn wants me. I thought for sure she did. "Why won't you talk to me?" I sound pathetic.

Her jaws knead at her tongue. Her eyes skim the sockets, slightly off as if she might pass out. "I . . . am . . . trying. Hard . . . after . . . go dark."

"I'm sorry. I'm so sorry." I'm going to cry for real if I don't keep moving. I swig down the last of my coffee and get the keys and crush another sob. It reverberates in the hollow of my chest.

As we get into the car, she squeezes my hand. "New variants," she says.

"I don't . . ."

She cups my hand in hers. "I want . . . to show . . . something."

The drive takes an hour.

Dawn gives directions with the merest gesture. Out of the city, past the suburbs where she lives with the stepfather who hates her, past a green field of wheat, and onto a gravel road that dives into the forest. I have the sense of driving through a snapshot of her life. That she wants to share it with me eases the pain in my chest a little.

"Slow down."

The car inches past a long expanse of chain-link fence. Everything inside is decrepit and decayed. There are several heaps of rusted metal. Once they might have been cars or tractors. Where other people would have a lawn, weeds grow in thick clumps dotted with trash—fast food bags, empty cans, oil bottles.

A big-headed, thick-chested dog with a brindled coat guards the fence.

Dawn points to the mailbox as we pass and says, "Hobart."

"What is this place?" I ask. "Who's Hobart?"

"Asshole."

"Do you want me to stop?"

She waves me on and has me park a quarter of a mile down the road. Apparently we have to walk back. Before we get to the edge of Hobart's property, we turn off the road, wading through thick undergrowth, some kind of fern, and a shrub with shiny, spiked leaves. When we are out of sight from the road, she leads me to the fence line. We walk along it, deeper into the forest.

"Are you sure we should be doing this?"

Dawn is scanning the lower edge of the fence, looking for something. I want to ask what, but the hunch of her body demands silence. I read her lines like I read Vadim, and I follow her, not wanting to go but unwilling to be left behind.

A couple of rotting sheds come into view.

Woven through the pine smell is the stink of meat and smoke and animal. As we approach the back of the property, the stench of urine and feces grows stronger. A rumble comes from deep inside the property. I can't place the sound, not mechanical, not the dog. It grows and turns into a growl. A shudder runs down my spine, and there's a hitch in my steps. We shouldn't be here.

I clutch Dawn's arm. "What is that? What's in there?"

"The hole, the hole, the hole." Dawn is muttering and fumbling at the fence.

The sounds seem to be coming from behind one of the sheds. I sidle down the fence, trying to see around the rotted siding. There's a cage of some kind. A dog run maybe, but the chain-link fencing is twelve feet high and covers the top too. What kind of an animal would be in a place like that?

"Shit."

I whirl around to see Dawn on her hands and knees.

"Shitshitshit."

She scrabbles at the dirt, digging with her fingers at the base of the fence. It's been reinforced. A piece of thick-gauge wire mesh has been fixed over the original hole. Pieces of quarter-inch rebar stake it to the ground. Her shoulders are hunched into her work, but even I can see there's no way she's getting through that part of the fence.

I lay a hand on her back.

I say her name like a prayer.

"Dawn—"

She whips toward me, clutching at me. "Have to get in."

My fingers lace through hers. I pull her to her feet. All I know is to wrap my arms around her shaking body and murmur promises no one can keep.

When she finally calms, I say, "What did you want to show me?"

She turns in the circle of my arms and points to the cage within the fenced yard.

At first, I see nothing except packed dirt and fencing.

It looks empty.

Then there's a huffing noise, a loud exhalation, and a dark bulk lumbers into view. It wheels toward us, smelling the air, and rises on hind legs. Rises and keeps rising—

A great black bear.

The size of the thing and its liquid, predatory motion terrifies me. Two perimeters of chain link separate us and they mean nothing. I hold Dawn closer.

"I don't understand," I say, reeling at the sight of a wild animal in a backyard pen. None of this makes sense.

"Hobart keeps her." Dawn's hands twist. A spasm starts in her shoulder and spreads, until her head makes a tic to one side.

"But why?"

The bear moves like storm clouds, pacing. Back and forth. Back and forth.

Dawn slips free from my arms and presses herself against the fence. From deep in her chest, I hear a low rumble that very nearly matches that of the bear.

The earth seems to shift under my feet.

There's Dawn and the bear and the way I dance for Vadim, and somehow these things are connected like moon and tide and ocean. But none of it quite fits together. There are too many barriers, so many cracks.

Dawn's fingers curl around the chain link, squeezing so hard her knuckles whiten.

The door of the trailer bangs open, and an old man comes out in nothing but boxer shorts. He scratches his balls and lights a joint.

I tug on the back of Dawn's shirt. "Let's go," I beg under my breath.

The old man inhales, holds in the smoke, and exhales in a cloud. He whistles a three-note call, and the dog slinks toward him. Its ears tilt our way. The dog has seen us, but he hasn't.

"Hobart." It's all Dawn says, but if the word were a spear, he'd be dead.

I pull on Dawn again.

This time she goes almost limp, and her hands slide off the fence. I half drag, half carry her away from the man and the dog and the bear. As soon as we're back in the car, she rummages through my bag without asking, finds a bottle of ibuprofen, and swallows four of them dry. She leans her head back against the seat and closes her eyes.

"We should report him," I say. "It can't be legal."

Dawn's sigh is more of a hiss. "Grandfathered in."

"It's animal abuse."

She's motionless.

"We have to do something!"

Dawn gestures for me to drive, and I put the car into gear, still seething. We slide past Hobart's mailbox, out of the forest, along the field, and to a house that doesn't feel like home. The last remnants of our childhood are slipping through our fingers.

DAWN

It takes three days for language to resume fully, for logical thought to quash the avalanche of sensory input. Looking back through the journal, nothing I wrote makes sense. An angry scrawl that cuts through the page in several places. Sketches of eyes and lines and landscapes that don't resemble any place I know.

After that, a single word, carved into the paper over and over and over again. *Fuckfuckfuck.* By the end, the letters are crushed together, a car wreck with casualties.

I close the journal like it might explode.

The cuts on my thighs are scabbed over.

I'm confined to the house because of the broken window and the ruined mimosa party. The way my mother is wounded by her unseemly daughter squeezes the oxygen out of my lungs. David is a truck waiting to run me down. The last fugue has left this body cracked open but within it I knew a place where I was boundless—notgirl, notDawn—but an extension of sky and soil, tooth and claw.

Coming back to these four walls feels like dying.

Except Jessie.

Hotlight, brightpoint. Jessie, the only place I know as home.

My mother says:
here are tickets
see her dance
you can go
ten days, ten more days

I am behind in my class and missed another discussion session.

Dr. Kerns is sending red-flagged warnings that my fast-track to Stanford in the fall is on the line.

Books are piled around my room.

Richard Dawkins. Stephen Jay Gould. E. O. Wilson. Old Chuck Darwin himself. I'm reading everything I can get my hands on about animal behavior, evolutionary theory, molecular genetics, and human evolution. There are seventeen search windows up on my computer screen. Mad skills in Boolean search. Fitness —we're talking about fitness. Who lives and who dies?

I intend to be an informed subject.

Dawkins says the body is nothing but a vehicle for genes.

It's the genes that hunger and want.

It's the genes that propel biodiversity.

The skinflesh is a failure if it can't launch a new generation.

This is what the biologists call fitness. The body survives. The body mates, spreads seed, pops out babies. This is the evolutionary success story. Simple, yes? Not on your life. Put fitness and genetic variation in the meat grinder of natural selection and the world is born.

There are parasitic flukes that cause ants to climb into the mouths of cows.

There are worms that make grasshoppers drown themselves.

There are fungi that transform ants into zombies.

I'm pacing again. Thinking and pacing. Ten to the window. Ten to the wall. Ten to the door.

My thoughts return to the bear. She has a few square feet of dirt and not one other fucking thing. She's an evolutionary dead end. Chain-link fence and Old Man Hobart have seen to that. She might as well be dead. From the perspective of evolution, she already is.

From: Dr. Stephen Kerns
To: Class Roster, OB-012 Advanced Topics in Animal Behavior
RE: Your next writing assignment

We've discussed microevolution, a measurable change in gene frequencies over time within a species. I hope you've had a chance to read each other's examples. The one on sticklebacks was particularly excellent. (Thanks, Mandy.) The real stickler (ha-ha) of course is translating this level of evolutionary change to the macro level—the origin of species.

For your writing assignment this week, define macroevolution and discuss how new species form. Due one week from today.

I am sixteen and I go to Alaska to visit my father and peer at the crumpled newborn face of my newest half-sib. We're invited to the pastor's house, an honor apparently, for lemonade and dessert and to view an educational presentation that reinterprets the fossil record.

This is important, *my stepmother says, cradling the baby.* There are so many misconceptions.

This is a documentary, *says my father.*

We watch over carrot cake with cream cheese frosting.

The goal of the film is to demonstrate that dinosaurs and humans coexisted. This is the linchpin of the six-thousand-year creationist timeline. It's careful work, this filmmaking. So-called experts make important observations over dinosaur track sites, and well-cut sequences with perfectly reasonable voice-overs present the Biblical leviathan as documented fact.

The pastor and his wife and my father and his wife and all the fathers and all the wives and all the children deemed old enough to grasp this important lesson are convinced. By the time a counter-expert is quoted saying, "Dinosaurs were extinct long before humans swung down from the trees," these nice, cake-baking people boo and hiss at the TV screen.

I consider sharing this choice tidbit of my past with Dr. Kerns.

From: Dawn McCormick
To: Dr. Stephen Kerns
RE: Macroevolution

Macroevolution is:
the formation of new species
an outgrowth of microevolutionary processes
a conundrum, like girls who hate pink

They say time heals all wounds. I'm not sure about that. But time also makes species. Eons, eras, periods (not the kind that require feminine hygiene products), epochs . . .
And separation.
That is a wound that cuts deep enough to sever a species in two.
The island fox is a gray-speckled, red-bellied, big-eared

carnivore. Cute enough to cuddle if you make it past the teeth. Sixteen thousand years ago (my apologies to my father's pastor), a couple of gray foxes from the mainland ended up on Santa Cruz Island off the coast of California.

Did they swim?

Catch a ride on a floating log?

Alien abduction and botched relocation?

Who knows? We weren't watching.

But once on the island, microevolution gets cranking. A mutation here. Another there. This one makes these foxes a little better at island life. Meanwhile back on proto-America terra firma, mutation chips away at the gray fox genome too. Change is the constant. And just like pulling a carrot cake from the oven, those wandering foxes who originally floated their way to the island have given rise to a whole new species. From *Urocyon cinereoargenteus to Urocyon littoralis*—macroevolution.

I turn in the assignment and almost immediately get a direct message from Dr. Kerns.

DrK: I do not want you to fail this class.

McCormick: Uh . . . thanks?

DrK: You have a very original mind.

McCormick: Tell that to my mother.

DrK: I have.

McCormick: What did she say?

DrK: She said that there were "issues."

McCormick: Of course she did.

DrK: I don't want to push you for details, but honestly, Dawn, you have so much to offer. I would love to see you at Stanford. It's the kind of place where a smart person like you could really thrive. And you've got the bridge program, a wide-open opportunity. All you have to do is pass this class. Think about it. Think about what you really want.

What I want.
What I want.
Does that even matter?

An hour later, I hear David's feet on the stairs, heading for my room. My mother is out, but before she left, she told him to make sure I don't leave the house. His presence on the other side of my door is a menace.

He knocks.

"What?"

The door opens. He takes in my room and finds it lacking.

"Filthy," he says, looking straight at me.

He makes me tired, this huge man with the small mind who fucks my mother. "Do you want something?" I ask, closing the book I am reading.

"You're failing your last class."

"How would you know?"

"Your mother set a grade alert."

Of all the things my mother has done, David might be the worst. I'm bristling and stabby. "Is she tracking my phone too?"

He smirks.

Enough of an answer.

"Did you know that there are lizards where every single individual is female?" His eyes get even smaller. If that's possible. "When the females ovulate, each egg has a full complement of DNA. Males are unnecessary to the species."

His face turns red. Science has that effect on some people.

"Do you know what the psychiatrist recommended?" he asks. It's a silverback maneuver. A chest-thumping challenge. When I don't respond, he answers anyway. "He says your presence in this family causes undue burden. He suggests antipsychotic medications and a secure group home placement. Your mother is considering it."

My chest cavity contracts.

Dr. Stubens has thrown me under the bus. "She wouldn't do that," I say, unable to keep the tremble out of my voice.

"She would if she thinks it's best for you."

"It's not."

He shakes his head. "Girls aren't supposed to act this way."

After he leaves, I sit on the bed shaking.

What I want is for him to get hit by a bus.

What I want is to stop being torn to pieces.

What I want is for things to make sense like they did when Jessie and I were girls.

I wonder what Jessie is doing right now. Opening night is just over a week away. I wonder if she knows what she wants. I wonder if her feet are bleeding. I want to run my finger over them. I want to know everything about her. I want Jessie to scare me.

Suddenly, in the midst of all this wanting, I remember.

In the last fugue, in the dayblind center of it—

There was pleasure.

The satisfaction of taking up space.

JESSIE

Tonight is opening night.

The dressing room is an avalanche of satin and tulle and whispered excitement. The younger girls are getting ready in front of one bank of mirrors. Those of us in the pre-professional program have commandeered the far side, applying makeup in thick swaths to our eyelids, our cheeks, and our lips.

It's hot under the lights, and our faces gleam. The air is thick with hairspray and deodorant and powder.

"Will you zip me?" Lily holds the bodice of her costume against her chest and turns around. The band of her tights hugs her narrow waist. Her back is smooth. The rich purple fabric against her dark skin reminds me of the sky just after the sun sets. She lets out a breath as soon as the zipper is up and smooths out the layers of tulle that fall to mid-calf. "Do I look okay?"

"A little lipstick right there," I say, tapping my front tooth.

She swipes it with a finger. "Gone?"

I nod. "You look perfect."

"You look like a cobra," she says, grinning so I know it's a compliment.

Vadim has gone with pared-down costumes in solid black to emphasize the body. The single garment is a leotard and tights combined. It has a halter top that clasps behind the neck and a plunging back and sheathes our legs completely. Even our pointe shoes are black so the audience will perceive a seamless line of shape and motion. He sent someone in earlier today to braid our hair into coils that snake along the back of our heads.

Brianna pushes her way front and center in the mirror, using Mimi's lipstick like she owns it and making a production of adjusting the straps on her costume.

"I hear that you're practically having sex onstage," she says, smirking.

I ignore her and finish my eyeliner.

Mimi reclaims her lipstick. "You wish it was you," she mutters.

"Yeah," says Nita. "You're the porn lover." She moans and pumps her pelvis in Brianna's direction.

Brianna lifts her chin and acts all prim and proper. "It's Eduardo who matters for our careers. Too bad there wasn't room for any of you in *Four Variations*."

"We're heartbroken," I say.

"At least we don't look like we're doing a school recital." Nita makes a point of going back to yet another application of mascara. Her eyes are black holes.

Brianna splutters, but before she can say more, the stage manager, a dour woman with a beaked nose, pokes her head through the door and shushes us. "Five minutes until curtain, girls."

The younger dancers' excitement goes up. Those of us who have been dancing for longer, for whom more is at stake, fall silent, focusing on our last-minute preparations. *Turbulence* is up right before intermission. Typically the oldest and most accomplished dancers would all be at the end of the program, but Eduardo determined the order for the showcase. In a not-so-subtle snub to Vadim, Eduardo's own piece is the last one the audience will see. They will go home with the sweet, classical steps of *Four Variations* on their minds.

I check my makeup one more time in the mirror, smear a bit of Vaseline on my front teeth, and think of the six-foot-tall stripper. I'll need to channel some of her mojo tonight.

I duck into the wings where I can warm up and watch the first three pieces.

The house lights dim, and the crowd grows quiet. Stage lights illuminate four dancers from the advanced class. They are swathed in white feathers for the "Danse des Petits Cygnes" from the second act of *Swan Lake*. The audience is rapt as they execute the initial sequence of pas de chat in unison. These four are good. They'll be moving into the pre-professional program this summer.

I'm so intent on my analysis that I don't realize Vadim is behind me until he lays his hands on my shoulders.

"Are you nervous?" he asks, leaning in so close that his lips brush my ear. Desire throbs through me, a deep wanting so powerful that I might burst. I turn to face him. He's shirtless and wearing black tights. It's minimalist and effective. A massive tattoo of a swarm of bats swirls up the left side of his chest and over his shoulder. "Tonight you must commit fully to the dance."

"Isn't that what I've done?" I whisper.

The stage manager shoots us an irritated look.

Vadim pulls me away from the wings and into the darkness backstage. He presses his body against mine, and the heat of him is sex-charged. He runs his hands down my side, skimming my breasts, coming to rest upon my hips.

"When you forget that people are watching, you are ferocious," he says.

The smell of him seizes me. I clutch at the muscles of his back and tip my face to meet his mouth. Before our lips touch, there is a commotion in the wings. We remember where we are. He squeezes my hips once then disappears into the dressing room. Craving knocks the wind out of me.

A moment passes before I notice Selene on the other side of the stage. She is wearing street clothes. Her hair falls in waves around her shoulders. All the pieces fall into place with deft precision.

She came to watch Vadim perform.

And she has seen us.

DAWN

My mother is wearing too much perfume and talking too loudly. I'm grateful when the theater goes dim. I sit through the dances. Girls, featherthin, dressed as birds. A waltzing ring of rosy-cheeked peasants in flower crowns. Boys who leap on legs made of springs and rubber. I sit in the smothering dark, waiting for Jessie.

JESSIE

As the curtain falls on the piece before *Turbulence*, the crew rushes to change the set.

Selene has disappeared in the backstage chaos.

There's a rushing in my ears, and I need an excuse to offer Selene. I can tell her it was part of the dance. I can tell her it was a mistake. But that has to wait.

Turbulence is coming.

Our backdrop—a thin scrim printed with a collage of Thom's sketches and lit from behind—settles into place. His drawings of us are layered. Some torn and the pieces separated. Others enlarged to giant size. The charcoal lines flow into one another. A breast, a hand, a hip. Yearning and resistance. Comfort and loneliness. A turbulent history of bodies in motion.

Nita and Mimi find their marks behind the curtain. They sit splay-legged on the not-quite-square forms at stage left and stage right. Vadim takes center stage. He is waiting for me to join him, but I'm turned to stone by the realization that both my excuses are true. Our attraction is part of the dance, and my mistake was thinking it was more than that.

He beckons me with a violent sweep of his hand.

The stage manager prods me.

I elbow her away.

Suddenly I am exquisitely aware of my body—its strength, its desire.

I close my eyes and I'm in the forest with the bear.

She is under my skin, and I am in hers.

Savage, feral, fierce.

There is only one difference.

She cannot get out of her cage.

My eyes snap open.

I take center stage and rise en pointe.

Vadim wraps his hands around my waist.

All the lights go off.

The audience quiets.

The curtain rises in darkness.

I breathe in rosin and dust and summon my own wildness.

I will make them burn.

The lights and music explode simultaneously at full volume, and the crowd flinches. Immediately I twitch into an arabesque. My leg cuts an electric, jagged slash through the air. Vadim lifts me, and I crumple around his arms only to be thrown outward.

Startled cries rise from the audience.

Only our clasped hands and the counterweight of our bodies keep me from falling. I launch myself into space. Vadim pulls me back, salacious and hungry. My legs scissor around his hips, and he holds me there. My crotch is crushed against his, and my want equals his own until once more we move apart.

I spin toward Nita, exploding into a storm of arms and legs. She catches me, stops me from blowing to pieces, and enfolds me in the curve of her body. My rib cage heaves, pressing against her breasts, and we stay connected, moving across the stage like we are one person. Her hands slide the length of my body. We reach together, lengthening until we are an axis for the turning sky.

When the music changes, so do we.

Our longing is no longer coincident, and we dance all the ways people shatter one another. Mimi and Vadim and Nita and I ricochet across the stage. Bullets. Fists. Blades. And I hate them. I hate being alone. I hate being confined. I hate out-of-control. We slam against one another. Hitting and recoiling.

Just as suddenly we find our way again. We come together. The music doesn't slow but we do. Mimi sweeps into arabesque and leans into space. Nita wraps her arms around Mimi's elevated leg and will not let her fall. I orbit until Vadim reaches out his hand and reels me in. I twist into Mimi. Nita insinuates herself among our limbs.

We are all connected.

Arm to leg. Hip to chest. Head to hand. I am face to face with Vadim. A rivulet of sweat snakes down the middle of his chest.

The music ends as abruptly as it began.

In the light booth, the tech kills the spots.

We vanish into darkness.

DAWN

Jessie, Jessie, Jessie. De-boned and unbound. One leg launching, impossibly high, long, slick. She is the curvature of the earth, an invitation, a challenge. Pound and thump. Storm and calm. Upheaval, migration, an ocean of grass. Heartbeat and hooves. Fur and claws. Pushpullpush. Letting loose not holding back. Ignition. Flame. Conflagration.

JESSIE

For a split second, only the furious thumping inside my ribs exists, and then the audience rises to its feet, shocked and unsettled, finally applauding in a growing tumult. Exhilaration pulses through me. I am unbridled, debrided, and reborn. What matters is not what is taken but that we fight.

DAWN

A thousand hands rumblethunder. The noise reverberates through me. On the stage . . . Jessie. Untouchable. The house lights come up. My mother babbles. I stare at the closed curtains, stare at the stage where the girl I knew transmogrified. She has pierced me with wildness. She is a beast on the hunt, a wolf bitch snarling. I am incinerated. Gone.

JESSIE

Backstage, Vadim pumps his fist in the air. The tattooed bats dart across his chest. The other girls congratulate us. Even Brianna. I buzz with electricity. My muscles burn, and I think I must be glowing from the inside out like a star going supernova. I soar through intermission on adrenaline and the seething chaos of the dance.

This body—my body—mine.

When intermission ends and the stage manager hisses for silence, I go into the dressing room and check my phone, hoping for a message from Dawn. There's nothing. I wish she could have been here. I wish we could have shared this.

I watch *Four Variations* from the wings. The other girls are a field of flowers in their purple dresses. The music begins slowly, lyrically. Their arms rise and fall in unison. The tulle of their skirts cascades from uplifted legs. Lily and Caden dance their pas de deux in the center of the other dancers. He lifts her, and she seems to float, ethereal above the stage.

She is going to be as good as Selene someday.

She will dance *Swan Lake*.

And I don't hate her for that.

I see Eduardo on the other side of the stage.

I don't hate him either.

When I'm back in street clothes and the heavy makeup is wiped from my face, I slip through the stage door with my bag over my shoulder. Families fill the sidewalk outside the theater. I look for my parents, half hoping that I won't find them. Little girls in fancy dresses clutch bouquets and squeal when they find their big sisters, still flushed, carefully leaving on their stage makeup so everyone will know that they are ballerinas.

People shift away from someone cutting through the crowd with a strange, almost inhuman, gait. There's something off about the set of the shoulders, the pendulum of the arms. It makes them nervous, but when she turns toward me, scowling, I've never been so happy to see anyone in my life.

"Dawn!" I cry, racing toward her.

When she sees me, her face changes completely. The scowl vanishes. She lives up to her name, sun rising. She weaves toward me and we embrace.

"I didn't know you were coming!" I say.

Dawn holds me more tightly but doesn't speak.

When we separate, I feel giddy, drinking her in. "You dressed up," I say. It's shocking to see her like this in tight black trousers and a crisp white shirt, unbuttoned to the rise of her breasts. "Fancy pants."

She scowls again, picks at her cuff, and I giggle.

Suddenly, her mother is there, in a flushed panic.

Dawn stiffens.

"I was looking everywhere," her mother snaps.

"Where would I have gone?" Dawn asks in a monotone.

Her mother shifts uncomfortably and doesn't answer. Instead, she turns her overexuberant attention on me. "You were very intense, Jessie. Wow! I can't believe we forgot to bring flowers. Dawn has been so excited to see you dance."

"Mother . . . ," Dawn growls.

Monica's lips pinch shut.

The stage door opens again, and the noise of the crowd increases. Every woman within a ten foot radius quivers like a tuning fork. Everyone except Dawn. It's Vadim, of course. He signs programs and kisses cheeks, leaving starstruck girls with their fingers pressed against the warmth left by his lips. Even Dawn's mother stares. He is impressive. I'll give him that.

"Did he hurt you?" Dawn demands.

"What? Vadim? No."

And he didn't. I played the game. I went all in.

Before I can say anything more, he's looming between us. "Spectacular, Jessie. Marvelous! Everyone is talking. You made my choreography roar."

Selene glides toward us and nestles herself against Vadim. She beams up at him. "You were fabulous!" she trills. The airy lightness of her tone is as much of an illusion as her own delicacy.

Vadim's eyes flicker between us, settle on Selene. "You think so?" His accent rolls off the tongue, another round in the game. She places her tiny hand on his chest.

"Delicious," she says, lapping him up like a kitten with milk.

When he pauses to sign an autograph for Dawn's mother, Selene pulls me aside. Every single part of my body tenses. What am I going to say to her?

She reaches toward me.

My flinch is involuntary, but it amuses her. Selene puts the flat of her hand against my cheek and pats it one, two, three times. Not a slap but none too gentle either. "You are a good dancer," she says. "Very good. And I'm sure, knowing Vadim the way I do, that he thinks you'd be excellent in other ways." She dissects me with surgical precision. "But Vadim will use you to get what he wants, and then—" She pauses, holding the moment the way she holds the audience when she dances Giselle. She lets me fill in the blank.

Vadim extricates himself from Dawn's mother and drapes an arm over Selene's shoulder. He congratulates me one more time. She flashes me a radiant smile, and they disappear into the crowd.

"Well—" says Dawn, frowning. "I guess she didn't like you macking all over her man."

"I didn't mack all over him!"

"Uh . . . yeah you did."

Before I can give Dawn a hard time, her mother's expression changes. She looks like she's going to be sick. I follow her eyes and see my parents heading toward us. My mother cradles a huge bouquet of calla lilies. My favorite.

She wraps her arms around me, crushing the flowers between us. "I'm so proud of you!" she says, beaming.

Then she notices Dawn.

Her face shifts. I watch her struggle to place those freckles, that sturdy frame. A second later, recognition and disbelief are at war on her face. "Dawn?" she says, one hand reaching out.

Behind her, my dad makes a strangled sound.

And there they are, my parents and Dawn's mom, glaring at each other.

It is not a pretty sight.

My mom breaks the silence. "Monica."

The name is brittle on her tongue.

Dawn's mother flushes bright red but lifts her chin and stands tall like she is expecting much worse. "Lauren. Joel. It's been a long time."

My father coughs, and my mom shoots him a death glare. "Did you know that she would be here?"

"Of course not." My dad looks like he hopes the sidewalk will crack under his feet and suck him down.

Dawn catches my eye and mouths *I'm sorry.*

I shrug and give her a weak smile.

"Time to go, Mother," says Dawn, tugging on the strap of Monica's purse. To me, she says, "You kicked ass tonight. Really."

I hug her again and whisper in her ear, "I really wanted you to be here."

She grins and saves the day, dragging her mother away from mine before things get uglier. As soon as they're gone, my mom insists we leave. "Joel," she snaps, and my father falls into step behind us. "Do you still want to eat at the sushi place?" she asks, without a backward glance.

"Sure," I say.

She turns at the next corner, speed walking. No one speaks for a block and a half.

Finally, my mom says, "You could've mentioned that the dance was going to be so . . ."

"What?" I snap. "So slutty?"

"I didn't say that."

"Then what?"

"I didn't think modern dance was your thing."

"Maybe it is now," I snap.

"Your friend Lily was lovely in that last piece."

My friend, Lily?

I've mentioned her a couple of times on the phone.

In a single sentence, Mom has all but erased Dawn. I'm mad in more ways than I can count.

"You had no right to keep me away from Dawn."

My mother's face hardens. "It wasn't about you."

I stop walking. Dad nearly runs into me. My mom turns to face us. This is my family, and I am tired of avoiding things. "She was my best friend," I say. "And you ruined everything."

My mom makes an ugly sound. She glares past me and fires on my dad. "Monica was my best friend."

My dad rolls his eyes. "Eight years," he says. "Can't you let it go? Can't you accept an apology?"

I watch her face going nuclear and decide to evacuate the fallout zone.

"I'm going now," I say. "You guys have to figure this out. I'll be at Patrice and Ed's."

They don't try to stop me.

DAWN

I lift the window, lean out until the sill presses hard against my stomach. Rain has started. Drops pelter my face, carrying the nighttime scents of writhing things, slick leaves, and bitter berries. Thoughtshards. Quickcut. I'm reaching for something. I feel it there in the depths like a monster waiting to surface. The pieces must fit together somehow—

> Jessie on stage, ferocious
> a bear in the forest, caged
> the center of the fugue, a refuge

This is where the answer lies. I reach for my mother's makeup mirror. I am going to induce another fugue. The journal is open on my desk. I make notes. There are things I need to know. On my laptop, I activate the camera, but before I press record, the phone rings.

I know it's Jessie.

No one else calls me.

"Did I wake you?" she asks.

I manage a grunt, try to get a hold of language.

"It's so late. I must have. I'm sorry, but I had to talk to you."

She is agitated, rambling. My answer is a halting conglomeration of words: "Night sounds. Rain. Who can sleep?"

"Exactly!" She is enthusiastic like a little girl.

"Watching you," I say. "A transformation."

"I wanted you there so badly and there you were, like magic!"

This makes me swell and burstsmile, hothappy.

She keeps talking, and I don't want her to ever stop.

"Did you hear the audience gasp at the beginning?" she says. "I think we shocked them. I love that." I shut the laptop and turn off the lighted mirror. I'm not ready to leave her yet. "But, oh my god, our parents. That was the worst. You should have seen . . . after you left . . . oh my god, my parents. Disaster."

"Jessie," I say, edging in. "You sound too happy."

"I do, don't I? That's so goofy. It was horrible, but you know what? I left them. I just left them there in the street. And you know what else? I am not going back to Olympia. Not ever again. I don't care what they say."

"What comes next?"

"I don't know. Something wild. Something of my own making."

She is incandescent through the phone, and I bask in her.

"We have performances through next weekend. After that . . . either I stay here with the company or . . . I don't know . . . we could run away to San Francisco. I can dance there, and you can go to Stanford. How about that?"

When we finally hang up, I decide to try and salvage my grade in Dr. Kerns's class, because San Francisco and Jessie and blanket forts and fairy dust could be the answer to everything.

JESSIE

I'm still buzzing when I get to the theater the next day. As I head into the dressing room, the grouchy stage manager actually smiles at me, which I don't understand but do appreciate. Mimi and Nita are already there, outlining their eyes in black.

"Did you see it?" Nita says as soon as I walk in the door.

"See what?" I ask, changing into my costume.

Mimi rolls her eyes. "You are so dense."

"Don't be cryptic."

"Don't be a bitch," says Mimi, handing me a folded section of newspaper.

There's a picture of Vadim and a review:

Under normal circumstances, student performances are not reviewed, but this year's showcase, danced by the most advanced students in the upper school at Ballet des Arts, marks principal dancer Vadim Ivanov's choreographic debut.

A stark departure from the classical focus of the company, Ivanov's creation, a piece entitled Turbulence danced by four dancers including Ivanov, is modern and raw. His decision to use student dancers was brilliant. Their rough-hewn skills articulate his exploration of attraction and repulsion in stark relief. This ballet is not beautiful. In fact, at times, it is downright ugly. Some may object to the intensely sexual content, especially when danced by underage ballerinas, but it is, nonetheless, a performance not to be missed. You might hate it, but you definitely shouldn't miss it.

The rest of the program exemplifies what Ballet des Arts does best—the clean, elegant lines of classical choreography. Four Variations, danced by the pre-professional students and directed by Eduardo Cortez, showcased fifteen-year-old Lily Michaels, who is most definitely a dancer to watch. Ballet des Arts will have several openings in the corps de ballet this season. Michaels would be a welcome addition. Not since current principal Selene DePriest joined the company has there been such promise in one so young. We can only hope there will be more performances from Michaels in the years to come.

I toss the paper on the counter and get to work on my makeup.

"Well?" Mimi demands.

I stop with the mascara. "Well, what?"

"He called us ugly!"

I shrug. "The dance is kind of ugly and violent and amazing all at the same time. At least it's saying something real."

"He called us rough-hewn," says Nita. "What does that even mean? It's not like we're two-by-fours."

I think about this as I tape my toes. I have bent myself to match the shape of ballet, to fulfill what I thought it required. Dancing with Vadim has cracked something open in me. It's liberating and I want more of it. But this piece—*Turbulence*—it is still his work, his vision. We are still his raw materials.

Lily arrives and the other dancers in *Four Variations* give her dirty looks. They're pissed that she was singled out in the paper. I should be jealous of her, too. The reviewer might as well have announced her selection to the corps, but I don't have it in me anymore.

"Hey," I say, giving her a hug. "Congratulations. That was an awesome review."

"You're not mad at me?" she asks, noticing a particularly nasty look from Brianna.

"I'm not going to be the one to tear you to pieces," I tell her, and I leave the rest of them in the dressing room so I can warm up backstage. I've spent the last year working as hard as I could at Ballet des Arts. Eduardo will pick me or he won't. Either way I'll figure it out, but tonight I'm dancing *Turbulence* and I sure as hell intend to dance it full out.

No mirrors. No more analyzing.

Full on ugly.

DAWN

Circadian rhythms are:
animal activity, both physiological and behavioral
driven by the light-dark cycle, sunrise, sunset
twenty-four hour periodicity
regular change, blood cadence, heartbeat

They are called chronobiologists, those that study time. These scientists are active in the daylight hours—diurnal. The owls and late-night humans, mostly musicians—nocturnal. The plants, too, respond to the cycling of Earth on her axis, spreading leaves, opening blossoms, calling to their beetle friends.

Matutinal: active during the morning

Vespertine: active at dusk

Crepuscular: to sleep in the highday and in the deadnight and to take the twilight hour and the dawn and make it yours. This is the bear—crepuscular.

And then there is me:
waking at firstgraysky, needing to roam
highnoon takes me like a shooter, deadtired
dusk, the infinite hour

4:23 a.m. I wake, begin recording my body temperature and pulse rate at three-minute intervals.

7:55 a.m. Automated reminder: Online discussion for OB-012 Advanced Topics in Animal Behavior begins in five minutes. This is a problem for my data collection protocols. I log in to the classroom chat with a thermometer hanging out of the corner of my mouth.

DrK: Hello, everyone!

MandyJ: Hi!

Xtra: What up, peeeple?

BigDuane: Dude.

Lori: Here.

Shane: Here.

McCormick: Present.

DrK: Simple question today: Is evolution occurring in the human species?

Lori: You mean like now?

DrK: Yup. Remember, you've had some readings related to this. Each of you was supposed to read at least two articles on the list. Should be some good examples we can discuss.

MandyJ: I read the one about how medical intervention has relaxed selection.

DrK: Excellent. Did anyone else read that?

Shane: Yup. Big-headed babies on the rise.

DrK: Why don't you two explain a little more?

MandyJ: The ultimate selective force is death, right? If you die before reproduction, your genes don't get passed on to the next generation.

Shane: But now we have all this amazing medical

technology like C-sections. Babies survive that would have died in the past because their heads were too big.

Lori: So why aren't we all walking around with giant heads?

BigDuane: You're kind of a fat-head. Did your mom have a C-section?

DrK: Cool it.

BigDuane: *puppy eyes*

Xtra: Maybe we will have giant heads in ten thousand years.

Shane: There also has to be an advantage to bigger heads.

Lori: Bigger brains should be better, right?

BigDuane: Tell that to the cockroach.

MandyJ: Don't forget that the moms used to die too, if the pelvis was too small for the baby.

DrK: Any other examples of medical intervention that might relax selection?

MandyJ: Glasses.

Shane: Dental work.

Lori: I had an appendectomy when I was twelve.

DrK: So does all this mean we are not evolving as a species?

Shane: If one trait was favored in the past (say medium head size in babies), changing the pattern of death means evolution goes in a new direction, not that it just stops.

DrK: Reread that, people. Shane has identified something important.

McCormick: What about time?

Xtra: It's time for coffee.

DrK: It is always time for coffee.

Xtra: *fistbump*

DrK: But I want to know more about what McCormick is getting at. Tell us about time.

McCormick: Time is critical on all levels. It structures global patterns: think El Niño, glacial melt, tidal flux. It drives animal behaviors: foraging, mating, hibernation. It is a requirement of evolution: change in gene frequency over time. Don't you see. It's about scale. Humans might make the clocks, but time is steamrolling us.

Shane: That's a little bit melodramatic, isn't it? Especially for someone who keeps missing class.

DrK: Give me more, McCormick. Explain in terms that we've been using.

McCormick: Typically we think of evolution happening over tens or hundreds or millions of years, but technology is changing in months. Culture is changing fast too.

DrK: Why is that important?

McCormick: We're bags of genes, right?

BigDuane: Hey! Watch the insults, McCormick.

McCormick: Selective pressures that drive evolution come from our environment.

Lori: I see where you're going with this. We are changing our own environment so quickly. Can evolution even keep up?

Xtra: Shit, man. When evolution can't keep up, it's dark days . . .

BigDuane: And dead dinosaurs.

McCormick: Physicists can't figure out time. Why is it the only irreversible force? Why doesn't it work the same way in the calculations of relativity as it does on the quantum scale? Time is both a human and a physical construct. What happens when we lose time? What if the only response—other than extinction—to the problem of *Homo sapiens* surviving in such a rapidly changing world is saltatory evolution?

DrK: Hold up, McCormick. We haven't gotten to this in the readings. CliffsNotes for the rest of you. Saltatory evolution is the hypothesis that mutations in one or a few regulatory or developmental pathway genes can lead to large and dramatic changes in physical traits. Some biologists believe that new species form this way.

McCormick: Exactly! We could be changing right now. Maybe we're the future. A new branch on the hominid family tree.

DrK: That is probably taking things a step too far.

McCormick: Not if you knew what I know . . . Shit . . . I forgot to take my temperature again . . .

DrK: McCormick? On topic, please.

McCormick: My physiology is exactly what we're talking about here.

JESSIE

I have not seen Dawn since opening night, four days ago. I've hardly even heard from her. A text now and then. Then today, just before the performance begins, she sends a video. It's a news clip filmed at the Copenhagen Zoo. First, it shows a two-year-old giraffe standing behind cable fencing. It is all stretched lines, an impossible animal, elegant and slipshod at the same time. The newscaster explains the complicated calculations of zoo breeding genetics. This animal is too similar to others in the herd. If she were to mate, inbreeding would be severe.

This explains the cull.

The giraffe is fed a last meal of rye bread and then shot and fed to the lions in the next pen over. Children watch. It is a gruesome dissection.

Before I can decide how to respond, my phone blows up. Text after text pours in from Dawn. It's a litany of death. Pictures of rhinos slaughtered by poachers. An orangutan killed during a botched surgery. A cougar lethally removed from an Atlanta suburb. Captive wolves starved to death by a country music star too busy to feed them.

I'm assaulted with carcasses.

When the carnage stops, I still see blood and empty eyes and death.

And then Vadim calls me.

It is time to dance.

DAWN

From: Dr. Stephen Kerns

To: Dawn McCormick, Student ID # 91967

RE: Erratic behavior

Ms. McCormick,

It pains me to write this e-mail.

You are precisely the kind of student with whom I most enjoy working. Too many minds become entrenched in preconceived notions about how the world works and what things mean. I value your risk-taking and free-thinking. I think both will serve you well no matter what you pursue.

That said, I am bound by the necessity of following my own rules as much as I wish I could bend them. You have missed multiple discussion sessions and your responses to written assignments have been unconventional. At this point, it will be impossible for you to achieve a passing grade. After your outburst in the last discussion group, I have decided to drop you from the class rather than give you an F, which would stay in your record.

I sincerely hope that you find what you are looking for and that you continue to pursue science in another setting.

Best,
Dr. Kerns

The pain starts in my hands. The fingers lock into claws. I stare at them, twitching in my lap. My cells have turned. There will be no blanket forts, no glitter falling from the sky.

JESSIE

The showcase sells out. It's a first for Ballet des Arts. Usually, the only time the company packs the house is during *Nutcracker* season. Instead of the typical small group of friends and family gathered outside the stage door after each show, there's always a crowd.

Word about Vadim's choreography is drawing modern dancers and performance artists, burlesque performers and parkour enthusiasts. Even his tattoo is getting top billing. Women want to run their fingers across the wings of bats.

He lets them.

The reviewer returns and writes a profile of Vadim for the arts section of the paper. Vadim is milking his rock star status and needs us to complete his ensemble. A television crew comes midweek and sets up before the evening performance. The producer and the reporter, a willowy woman in a blue dress, are talking with Vadim about the plan for the shoot. There are two cameramen getting set up. Camera people? One's a woman, and she nods as she feeds cable across the stage.

"Don't trip," she says, the only person who seems to notice that Nita, Mimi, and I are animate objects rather than another piece of stage dressing. Our stage manager lowers our backdrop and moves the forms into place on the stage. Vadim's shirt is already off.

The producer is impatient. "Over here, girls."

Nita bristles at being called a girl.

We pick our way around the new obstacles on the stage. We're fully costumed, and our instructions are to pretend like we are rehearsing in the background while Vadim is Vadim for the pleasure of viewing audiences everywhere. We pick a section that is low on the sex scale but high on weird.

"This feels so dumb," says Mimi.

Nita sweeps into a disjointed port de bras. "Living the dream."

"Okay. Quiet up there," says the producer. "We're going to get started."

The reporter opens things up and introduces Vadim. I rise and lower en pointe, pushing my arms forward and contracting my belly in a pulsing rhythm. I'm a heartbeat, a drum. Even without the techno backbeat, the syncopated steps have their way with me.

It's not until I sit on the stage right form and cede the dance space to Nita that I start to pay attention to the interview.

"You've certainly shaken things up in the dance scene here," says the reporter, looking like she wants to lay her hand right in the center of Vadim's chest. He laughs, not at all humble. "What's next for you?" she asks.

"The art, that's what's important." Vadim's accent is double-strong for the camera. "All I want is to be able to keep creating."

"With Ballet des Arts?" the reporter prompts.

"That depends on Ballet des Arts, doesn't it?"

If the rumors have any truth, Vadim might dethrone Eduardo and become the new artistic director of the company. The entire creative mission would change, and I could be at the center of it. That's an exciting thought.

"Given the success of *Turbulence*, do you think that the company will move in a different direction with its repertoire?"

"You'll have to ask our artistic director, Eduardo Cortez. He was kind enough to allow me space and dancers this spring." Vadim spreads his arms wide, displaying the tattoo to full effect and sweeping the rest of us into his grasp. I improvise a series of movements in place that will play well on TV.

"Ah, yes," croons the reporter, glancing over her shoulder at us. "Your young dancers have attracted a great deal of attention. How has it been working with students?"

Out of the corner of my eye, I can see Vadim considering us.

"They are willing to experiment."

The reporter appraises us. "Could you do more with professionals?"

Nita dives into a deep arabesque with her chest on my knee. "Bitch," she whispers. I try not to laugh.

"Technically, yes," says Vadim. "But viscerally—right here in the gut—I don't think so. Would you like to see how we work?"

The reporter is still gazing at his perfect abdomen. No doubt she'd like to get visceral. "Of course . . . ," she stammers, as Vadim leaves the camera's eye and interrupts us, clapping loudly.

"Excellent! Excellent!" he says, projecting to the back row of the theater. "You two take a moment." He waves Nita and Mimi toward the back of the stage and beckons to me. Both lenses swivel my way. The camerawoman gives me an encouraging smile. I take my place center stage and wait for Vadim's instruction.

I'm the little ballerina in the music box.

Open the lid and I spin.

"En pointe," he says.

I rise.

His hands slide around my waist. "Passé."

I slide my right toe up the side of my left leg until it is beneath my knee. My arms are rounded overhead.

"Attitude en avant."

I unglue my toe from my supporting leg and stretch it forward. As I do, Vadim turns me on an angle toward the left corner of the stage and repositions his hands at the small of my back for a lift. "Ready," he says, and like a gust of wind has swept me to the sky, I am suspended above his head. My back arches. Both legs bend. I am all limbs and limber. Upside down I can see the reporter watching us.

In one motion, Vadim slides me down his chest and moves his hands so that I end up clasped in his arms, a classic fish dive. He sets me down and turns to the reporter, who claps for us.

Vadim holds up his hand. "Wait," he says. "This small dance. Very classical, yes? And so easy. I tell her the steps. She does them. But when I ask her to let go of the steps and to give me a thunderstorm instead, this is what happens."

He gestures for me to begin again.

I shoot into the passé, violent and jagged. My hips undulate, a growing wind. "Spin me," I say, and instantly I am a whirlwind beneath his hands. When Vadim stops me, I contract my abdomen, letting thunder ripple through me. My wrists and elbows snap into tight, unnatural angles. The attitude en avant is all broken lines and storm damage.

The second I hit my balance, he thrusts me into the air over his head. This time I am rigid rather than languid, a woman hit by lightning. The drop into the fish dive is so sudden it takes my breath away and when I'm crushed against his chest, I melt into the last desultory drops of rain before a storm clears.

There is no clapping this time.

Vadim sets me down in silence.

"That was incredible," says the reporter. "I don't even understand what I just watched."

Vadim puts his hands on my shoulders and tells her, "Jessie doesn't hold back. That's why it works. This is how we build the dance together."

DAWN

The mother—taptaptap. Red nails on the countertop. Sharp. Seeing her through glass. Smelling her through glass. Sweet, milky, bitter. She drinks, and the liquid slides down her throat. The body thrums. Wanting to stay. Wanting touch. Wanting to go. Itching to move. Yearning for distance. Far off smells— rain, worms, wetearth.

She gets up, leaves, no longer binds.

She is gone.

JESSIE

Before the last performance, I arrive early at the theater. Only the stage manager is here. She gives me a curious look but doesn't protest when I go to the stage instead of the dressing room. I pull out one of the foam forms from *Turbulence* and sit down in the center of the stage.

Empty seats stare back at me. Soon they will fill with people who see the surface of us. The graceful arc of Lily's arms and her easy smile. The tender duet that Mimi and Nita perform. The explosive crash of my body against Vadim's. They will watch the dancers ebb and flow, circle and sweep, oblivious to the blood and the Band-Aids and the Vaseline smeared on our teeth.

We are bodies.

It doesn't serve to overthink it.

Vadim said, *Jessie doesn't hold back. That's why it works.* Tonight I dance his choreography one more time. Selene said Vadim is using me. No doubt she's right. It's his dance, but not entirely.

Like Dawn said, we're changing.

Someday I will dance a story that is completely mine.

This is what I take into the performance that night. I am bestial, carnal, and brutal. I don't hold back. Everyone tells me that I am beautiful. They don't know what that means.

DAWN

In the woods. Hummingbuzzingcreaking. Wind sways the trees, hustles and rustles high above. The smell of livingdying expands with breath. Feet on mud. Fur on bark. Twigs scratchscratchscratch. There is new green. Shoots twining, reaching up. Leaves unfurling. Roots spreading. Spring burgeoning, impregnated. Promising, promising, promising . . .

JESSIE

The cast party is at a big, fancy house in the hills above town. Brianna's aunt owns it, and she's gone all out. There are cocktail shrimp in martini glasses with wedges of lemon, platters of cold cuts and fancy cheeses, and a cupcake tower. Plastic ballerinas are stuck in the pink frosting.

The others are giddy. There has never been a better showcase. *Four Variations* was spectacular. Eduardo said so. Maybe he will pick more than two new dancers.

I pluck one of the cupcake toppers from the tower and lick the frosting off the spike on the bottom. I roll the plastic girl between my thumb and forefinger and stare out the huge windows at the lit-up city. It's a clear night, and the river twists through the center of town far below me. The stern-wheeler, a passenger boat restored from an earlier time and festooned with lights, chugs slowly downriver. I imagine couples dancing inside to violins.

I watch Vadim offer Selene a glass of champagne.

The ballerina is an unnatural shade of pink. The color stamped on her face is askew, the paint not quite lined up with the pressed plastic eyeballs and lips. Her legs are fused together from thigh to pointe shoe. Poor thing can't walk. All she can do is spin around and around. I hold her by the feet and make her pirouette. Dance, little girl. Spin, little doll. Be pretty. Be sweet. I wonder why I ever wanted to be her.

My phone vibrates in my pocket.

It's Dawn.

Her name on the screen is a lifeline.

"Hello," I say, covering my other ear to hear over Brianna's vapid laughter. "Dawn," I say, "are you there?"

But it is not Dawn.

"Jessie, this is Monica."

She's scared. I can hear it in her voice.

"What's wrong?"

"I'm sorry. I . . . I didn't know who else to call. Is Dawn with you? Have you seen her?"

"She's not with me now."

"Okay then, I guess . . . I don't know. I . . . Sorry to bother you."

"Wait," I say. "Don't hang up." There is a long silence. This stupid party keeps getting louder. "Hold on. Let me go someplace where I can hear you." I slip into a guest bedroom and shut the door. "I talked to her the day before yesterday, and she seemed okay."

Monica is crying. "That was the day she left. I found her phone in her room with a note."

My heart is pounding in my chest. "What did it say?"

She reads in a halting voice: *I have been inside the alternative. It's okay, Mom. It really is. But I can't be what you want me to be.*

I fold the plastic ballerina in one fist and the edges of her tutu bite into my palm. "What happened when she left?"

"Did you know she blew her chance to go to Stanford?" Monica demands. I did not know this, but I don't give her the satisfaction of saying so. "She sabotaged an amazing opportunity. Who does that?"

"Mrs. McCormick," I say, trying to keep the anger out of my voice. "Did you do something?"

"I think . . . I know she heard me and David talking about finding another place for her to live . . . about hospitalization."

"You what?" I screech into the phone. "How could you do that to her? Why do you have to ruin everything?"

A strangled, incomprehensible sound comes from Monica.

"You're an awful person," I say.

"You know where she is, don't you?" Monica shrieks. "Tell me! Tell me right now or I'm calling the police."

"Screw you, Mrs. McCormick. Just like you do everything else."

I hang up and squeeze the plastic ballerina so hard that her legs snap.

I have to find Dawn.

I am not going to lose her again.

When I emerge from the guest room, the noise of the party slams against my eardrums. Brianna sways drunkenly into Caden. He catches her against his chest. It's a zoo in here. Too contained. Too loud to think.

I open the sliding door and step out on the deck. No one is out here, and the cold night air is a relief. I try to piece together where Dawn might have gone. We talked after the TV interview. I told her how Vadim had swaggered for the cameras. I told her about the rumors, about Eduardo and Vadim bashing heads.

She told me about a bird, some kind of grouse or something. The males puff out their chests and strut around one another, whooping and calling, for an audience of hens.

Shit. Where is she? It's freezing out here, and I left my pea-coat inside. Wherever she is, I bet she's cold too. I bet she's outside. She's always been happiest in the open—in our tree house, on a camping trip, sleeping in the hammock in my backyard. I know how she feels about walls and locked doors.

Out of nowhere, my stomach balls up into a tight, hard knot. I'm buried by images. It's almost as if, wherever she is right now, I'm inside of her. Seeing what she sees. Hearing what she hears. Knowing what she knows.

The zoo-born chimpanzee with her nose in a concrete corner.

The bloody giraffe, an unnecessary animal killed to feed the lions.

The orca holding her trainer on the bottom of the pool.

The bear in the cage.

There's a shrill buzzing in my ears.

I know where she is.

My heart is knocking on my rib cage like an ax murderer.

I know where she is.

I need a car and I need it now.

I know where she is.

I go back inside. Lily's mom gave me a ride here, but they've already left. The party feels even louder now. The colors swirl, chaotic. Mimi tries to pull me into a group of girls, but I need to go. This riot threatens to overwhelm the magnetic draw of an internal compass that points straight to Dawn.

I grab Nita by the arm and shout over the noise. "Do you have a car here?"

She shakes her head.

I scan the gathered dancers and their families. I don't know any of them well enough to borrow a car. A giddy peal of laughter catches my attention. It's Selene, sharing some private joke with Vadim.

Vadim—

He's a head taller than everyone else here, visible over the press of bodies. Even now, even in a rush to get to Dawn, the sight of him makes my pelvis throb with wanting. I'm long past expecting romance, but I know what it felt like to dance with him. I can't help imagining the sex.

Somehow he knows I'm watching.

Our eyes meet, and my breath catches.

He knows what I'm thinking too.

And I know that he'll help me.

I push through the crowd, shoving people out of the way. I cut in front of Selene and face him. "I need your car."

Behind me, an irritated huff escapes Selene. "You've got to be kidding."

But Vadim's brow furrows. He can read my face as well as my body. He nods his head toward the front door. "Wait for me out front."

To Selene, he says, "I'll be right back."

She argues, and he says something to her that I can't make out, and I don't care anyway. I grab my peacoat from the front closet and escape the party. I pace the front walkway. My mind is racing far ahead, out of this fancy neighborhood and into the dark place where I know I will find my friend.

I'm pulsing with anger. Mine or hers? I'm not sure, but underneath the fury, anxiety rises in me like a flood about to engulf a city. I must find her.

And soon.

The front door opens and shuts and Vadim is here.

"What's wrong, Jessie?"

He puts his hands in the pockets of his leather jacket and hunches his shoulders against the cold. For a second, I wish he would open his arms. I wish I could fall into them and be caught, but Vadim's not going to save me.

"My friend's in trouble. The one you've met a couple of times. She needs my help."

He stands close enough for me to smell him. "The one with the short hair?"

I nod.

"I remember her," he says. "She cares for you." His expression is soft. I've never seen him look like this. "A friend like that is a rare thing."

"Can I borrow your car? I have to find her before . . ." I can't complete the thought. My body won't stay still. It judders and twitches like a trapped animal.

Orca

Giraffe

Chimpanzee

How does the body respond to constraint?

Kill, be killed, or submit.

"Please," I beg. "I wouldn't ask, but I have no one else."

Vadim moves closer. He cups the back of my head in his hand and lays his lips on my forehead. "Be careful, love," he says, pressing a set of keys into my hand. He points to a black BMW parked at the curb and goes back into the party before I even have a chance to say thank you.

The heavy, powerful car glides out of the city and heads south. The freeway is a long stretch of gray nothing. It takes an hour to get to Dawn's neighborhood. This late at night, most of the windows in the identical houses are dark, but when I drive past her house, the kitchen is brightly lit, and I can see her mother walking back and forth, back and forth.

I drive out of the subdivision. Instead of turning toward the freeway, I turn the other way and go east, past the wheat field and toward the forest. The road turns to gravel, and I slow down, partly to protect Vadim's car but also so I can peer into the darkness on either side, looking for landmarks.

I check each mailbox looking for the name I remember.

At each turn, I let my instincts decide.

The road plunges deeper into the trees and goes for a long way without any driveways at all.

Then the fencing starts.

The chain link is old, bent in some places, broken in others. One particularly large hole is mended with a spiderweb of barbed wire. I stop and shine my phone light at the chipped lettering on the dented mailbox—*Hobart*. I pull into the driveway until I'm stopped by the padlocked gate. A sign with a bullet hole through it says *Beware of Dog*. Behind the fence I can see the sheen of the trailer's metal sides, but there are no lights on inside.

When I roll down the window, I'm engulfed in night sounds, the buzzing of insects and the chirruping of frogs looking for each other in the night. There's a rank undercurrent in the air, bloody, metallic, piss-tinged. I hear movement in the darkness on the other side of the fence. My pulse is a sledgehammer.

"It's just the dog," I tell myself, remembering the huge animal we saw when Dawn brought me here. "Just the dog. Just the dog." But I'm still scared. The chain link might as well be tin foil, and the sun is a long way from rising.

I don't want to open the car door. Anything could be out

there. I'm starting to think this was a bad idea. Maybe it was nuts to think I could find Dawn.

No one even knows where I am.

I open the glove box, looking for something like a weapon.

I find a plastic ice scraper and the car manual and a metal flask.

Vadim's emergency kit. I unscrew the lid and take a long swig of the alcohol inside. It's whiskey, I think, and it makes me cough. I crawl into the back, feeling under the seats for a tire iron or something. I dig through the pile of crap on the rear seat. A newspaper. Vadim's cashmere sweater. If only Selene's stuff were in here, she would probably have a can of mace. All he has is a leather messenger bag. I go through it anyway.

The press release is on top of a stack of papers.

Across the typed page, in loose cursive, it says:

This will appear in the arts section of the paper on Friday.
—Eduardo

The booze burns on the way down.

So does this.

For Immediate Release:

After nine years with Ballet des Arts, including the last three as principal dancer, Vadim Ivanov is leaving the company. He will be joining the world-renowned Ballet International based in Paris, France, as principal dancer and choreographer. According to Eduardo Cortez, artistic director of Ballet des Arts, Ivanov's departure is amicable.

"It has been clear for some time," said Cortez, "that Vadim's creative sentiments lie outside the purview of Ballet des

Arts. We hope this move allows him the freedom to explore his truly innovative, avant-garde sensibilities."

Ivanov's choreographic debut with Ballet des Arts this spring evoked strong reactions, both positive and negative, from audiences, but critics have been unequivocally enthusiastic about Ivanov's tense and biting modern ballet, *Turbulence*. About his move to Paris, Ivanov says, "I look forward to building a core group of dancers who are eager to work collaboratively and willing to take risks." When asked about what he plans to choreograph next, the rakish and often controversial dancer said only this: "We will continue to embrace the dangerous."

Cortez will be promoting current soloist Adam Williams to principal dancer. He also announced the two newest members of the corps de ballet, Lily Michaels and Caden Cross, both joining the company from the Ballet des Arts pre-professional program.

DAWN

A sound rises.
Metal, machine, an engine growls, surges, purrs.
The sound of open and close.
A voice.
A smell I know.
A smell I love.

JESSIE

I'm out of the car.

I don't remember opening the door.

The press release crumples and falls to the dirt.

I'm rattling the gate and calling for Dawn. Too loud, way too loud, in the night. The brindled dog rockets out of the shadows and crashes against the fence, a chaos of bared teeth and wild eyes and clamor. I recoil and slam hard against the hood of the car.

The air around me shifts, whips cold and hard on my face.

Instantly, the dog stops barking and stares past me.

A low growl reverberates from this side of the fence.

My skin crawls. The dog's nose twitches. Her ears flick back.

The growl comes again from a patch of shadow that's blacker than everything else. Oh my god the bear is loose. The bear is loose. The bear is loose. They will find my body in the dirt, in the dark, in this ditch. I am edging toward the car door. There's a loud huffing grunt and something moves in the bushes. I am fumbling for the door handle.

Fear electrifies me.

It's coming for me, for me, for me.

I tear open the door, thrust myself inside, and throw the car in reverse while my left hand is still scrabbling to pull the door shut. I shoot backward across the road. Way too far. The left rear wheel dips into the ditch on the other side. The car heaves underneath me, and I shift into drive before it can slide down the embankment.

I gun it.

Gravels flies in every direction.

The huge engine roars, and the bear lunges into the beam of my headlights.

A shriek tears out of me, burning my throat.

Bear.

Not bear.

Not bear.

Legs, arms, human.

My mind is churning, calculating, grasping.

Human.

I slam on the brakes. I'm swerving and screaming and cranking the wheel and screaming and screaming and stop, stop, stop.

Somehow I stop.

Somehow I don't hit her.

I don't hit Dawn.

I'm crying when she opens the door. I fling myself into her arms, and she holds me when my legs crumple. We tangle together, my face buried in her neck, and then I'm pulling her, clawing at her shoulders, trying to get her into the car.

"The bear, the bear. We have to go."

She wraps her arms more tightly and holds on.

She is too strong for me to struggle against.

"The bear," I shriek.

"Yes," she says. "Going."

"But . . . but . . ." I'm too panicked to get the words out. "There . . . back there . . . there's something . . ."

"Jessie."

"Dawn." I plead her name.

She smiles all white and sharp. "Me. You found me."

She releases my arms, reaches past me into the car, and turns the key in the ignition, silencing the engine. She puts the keys in her pocket and takes my hand, envelops my hand in her own. Her face is broader, her nose longer. The adrenaline, the fight or flight, the terror. Everything I sense seems distorted.

"Come," she says, leading me along the chain link and deeper into the forest.

The dog runs along the other side of the fence, no longer threatening. This is the way Dawn took me before. I recognize the sheds, the piles of junk, the cage. The back porch light of the trailer gleams into view. It illuminates the bear. She swivels toward us, huffs, and rises up on her hind legs. The pads of her enormous feet—bigger than my face—press against the fence. It curves outward. Steamy breath swirls in the cold air. Her mouth . . . those teeth . . . the tongue.

Dawn crouches and fumbles in the bushes.

I can't look away from the bear. Our eyes lock in a kind of dance.

There's a loud crack, and I break the gaze.

Dawn is kneeling on the ground with a pair of bolt cutters.

Another crack.

She is cutting through the fence.

"What are you doing?"

She ignores the question and cuts another section of wire. The dog whines and paws the ground where Dawn is working.

I'm still reeling from what happened on the road, but as rational thought returns, I am sure of one thing. We have to get out of here.

The wire has been snipped vertically about three feet up, and she keeps at it.

"Please," I beg. "Let's go."

She shrugs me off like a mosquito.

"What are you doing?"

She stands to get better leverage. There's a line of sweat down the center of her back.

"Say something."

She turns toward me so slowly that it is almost threatening, and I take a step back.

Dawn holds up the sharp instrument, inclines her head toward the cage. "The bear."

Another bolt of fear shoots through me. "You can't let her out."

A horrible snarl comes from deep in her chest.

My spine goes rigid.

"The cage, the cage, the cage," she rasps, a caustic litany that sears me.

"I know. It's terrible. It's bad and it's wrong and it's no way to live but we can't save her."

Dawn's face seethes. She's furious.

"I am so sorry," I stammer. "But if you let her out, they'll kill her. You know they will. They'll shoot her and dead is dead is dead."

A shudder racks her body like there's something inside her trying to burst out.

"Maybe that's better," she says.

"Maybe it is." I wrap my fingers around the handles of the bolt cutters. "But not at our hands. Not at yours. We couldn't live with that."

She stares at me for a very long time before she relinquishes the tool.

"We're taking the dog," she says.

I help her pull back the fencing until the hole is big enough for the animal to squirm through. She plants her front paws on Dawn's chest and licks her face all over. Such relief, a golden feeling, pours through me. The dog drops to the ground, circles me, and nudges me with her nose until I scratch behind her ears. Then she yawns and stretches and sits on her haunches.

"She needs a name," says Dawn. "You need to give her a good name."

Before we get in the car, I throw the bolt cutters in the bushes. There's a purple tinge to the sky in the east. The rest of the world will be waking up soon. I open the back door for the dog. She leaps in immediately, curls up on Vadim's sweater, and goes to sleep. Dawn slumps in the passenger seat. I drive past the entrance to the subdivision where Dawn's mother is. Even I know that we are not going there.

"Where are we going?" I ask.

She smiles without opening her eyes. "I am glad there's a *we* again."

"So am I."

Once upon a time our mothers tucked us in bed. Our fathers woke us up for school. Perhaps they thought we were no different from the china ballerinas I got on every birthday, tiny figurines who got dusted off and moved from stage left to stage right and back again. Rosy-cheeked and graceful, we were girls who did not bite or complain or wander.

After all, if we stepped out of line, they could knock us together and watch us shatter.

But we are not those girls any longer.

Not by a long shot.

"Take me into the mountains," she says. "The trees go on forever there."

I head south on the freeway until we can cut east toward the Cascades, a line of ancient, snow-covered volcanoes. On either side of the two-lane highway is a wall of forest. The strip of sky overhead is deep blue. Somewhere the sun is shining, but it hasn't found us yet.

No one has.

DAWN

everything inhales, exhales
moving toward, moving through
onward, forward
wildnew
feral
dawn

JESSIE

The sun is streaking through the treetops when we park at a trailhead leading up a steep slope. Dawn takes off without looking back. The dog seems content to walk at my side. My friend holds out her hands as she hikes, brushing the ferns with her fingertips, touching bark. She stops once at a fallen tree. Deep scratches and a pile of loose dirt next to the trunk are signs that something has been digging there. She crouches and rubs a pinch of soil between her fingers. As she stands, I see her lift her fingertips to her nose. When she moves on, there's something looser in her stride, an easy sway to her hips.

Exhaustion is catching up with me.

I haven't slept since yesterday morning.

It takes extraordinary effort for me to keep walking, but Dawn speeds up. There's a charged energy to her movements. Her strides grow longer, and step by step, she's outpacing me. We've gone so long without words, and I'm so out of breath, that it's an effort to speak. My voice cracks when I finally call her name. Thirty feet ahead of me, she pauses without turning, motionless in the middle of the path, as if startled.

"Dawn—" I say again.

Her head swings around, tracing a ponderous arc as if she's caught my scent. Our eyes meet, and there's a moment when I do not know her.

"I need to rest," I say.

And Dawn returns. Her limbs fall back into the shape I expect, and she comes back to me. We sit, thigh to thigh, on a fallen log. She's not even breathing hard. Trees tower around us, their tops swaying and murmuring. I pull my knees to my chest and rest my chin on them. Dawn scratches the dog absently, but she's still focused on the trail ahead.

"You're leaving," I say, suddenly understanding.

She leans into me. "We don't have to do what they say anymore."

There are thin rows of fading bruises on her arms. I touch them with one finger. "What is happening to you?" I ask.

Her answer slips out like wind over water. "I think you know."

"Are you safe?"

"Are you?"

Her expression is both tender and wild at the same time. I see the pulse in her throat and feel the heat of her. We have spent so long being careful. She kisses me hard and wet on the mouth. I crush her against me, slipping my hands under her shirt. When our lips part, I don't let her move away. I press our foreheads together.

"I don't want to lose you again," I say.

She pulls back so she can look at me. "We have everything to gain."

Before I can respond, she says, "Don't play it safe. Go back and talk to Vadim."

Dawn kisses me for the last time, soft, like we are made of the same flesh. The sun finally reaches us and pours down between the trees. Her lips leave mine, but I keep my eyes closed, drinking in light and warmth and the taste of her. When I finally open them, Dawn is loping up the trail, deeper into the woods. Steam rises from the damp earth. The air is golden and luminous. It reminds me of glitter and fairy dust, of us as girls and us now—pushpullpushing, fighting our way out.

Dawn is almost out of sight when her gait changes.

Her form shifts. She is muscle and movement, bulk and grace.

As she disappears into the trees, the last thing I see is a flash of nightblack fur.

ACKNOWLEDGMENTS

This book began with two images: a dancer taking off pointe shoes full of blood and a feral girl in the forest at sunrise. In a rather remarkable phone conversation, I told Andrew Karre that I intended to write about what it means to be a girl in a girl's body, and he said, "Yes." I'm grateful to him for going all in when I had not yet written a single word.

Alix Reid was the one who had my back as I wrote and rewrote and kept rewriting *Pointe, Claw*. I have been so blessed to have her editorial brilliance and her unwavering support as I clawed my way into this story. Her belief in me and Dawn and Jessie made all the difference.

I'm grateful to my supersmart writer friends for the pep talks and the manuscript critiques and their overall awesomeness. Thank you Addie Boswell, Martha Brockenbrough, Kiersi Burkhart, Melissa Dalton, Ruth Feldman, Jennifer Longo, Liz Rusch, Sara Ryan, and Nicole Schrieber for being my lifeline and my brain trust.

Fiona Kenshole is a lionhearted, honey-tongued super-beast of an agent. Without her I might be selling BodyBeautiful™ out of my basement. There are not enough ways to say thank you for all that she does on my behalf.

Authors need a lot of help. Lucky for me, I get to work with the incredible people at Lerner Publishing and at Transatlantic Agency. If they weren't so far away from Oregon, I would shower them in cupcakes every single day. Thank you!

As I write these acknowledgments, I am getting ready to head into the wilderness with my family. My parents, Marilynne and John, dressed me in overalls and let me call them by their first names. They bought my pointe shoes and took me to the forest. Thanks to them, being a girl meant I could claim the whole world. My husband, Seth, has an apparently unlimited capacity to tolerate the quirks of this writer. He weathers creative rants and blue hair and random crying jags with equanimity. Thanks to him I get to live, write, and play in a beautiful place. That was one well-placed kiss on the neck, sweetheart! Our children, Fisher and Beryl, are always up for adventure. They make me laugh and let me steal their one-liners and motivate me to be my best and truest self. They are the future and that makes me the most grateful of all.

ABOUT THE AUTHOR

Amber J. Keyser spent most of her fraught teenage years in a ballet studio, striving for perfection. She's always been intrigued (and frustrated) by the way the bodies of girls and women are the battlefield for culture wars—how we should look, who we should love, and how we should act. *Pointe, Claw* is an exploration of the territory of the body and her answer to the question posed by Mary Oliver: Tell me, what is it you plan to do with your one wild and precious life?

Amber is the author of *The Way Back from Broken* (Carolrhoda Lab, 2015), a heart-wrenching novel of loss and survival, and *The V-Word* (Beyond Words/Simon Pulse, 2016), an anthology of personal essays by women about first-time sexual experiences, among numerous other titles. Find out more at www.amberjkeyser.com.

PRAISE FOR

THE WAY BACK
FROM BROKEN

by AMBER J. KEYSER

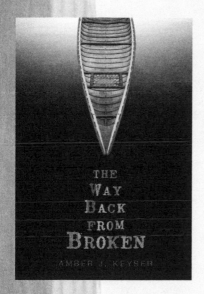

"[With] poignant relationships that never become schmaltzy, and a compelling high-stakes adventure, this vivid, moving exploration of grief and recovery hits all the right notes."
—starred, *Booklist*

"Rare in its honesty. . . . A subtly touching tale of liberation from grief that, with its sincere existential questioning, will stay with readers."
—*School Library Journal*

"A quiet and memorable story of how paddling in the wilderness forces two unlikely friends to face their grief and embrace their power."
—*Kirkus Reviews*

"This book is a heartbreaker, but any reader can benefit from its message of honesty, resilience, and courage."
—*VOYA*

An Assembly on Literature for Adolescents of the NCTE (ALAN) Pick